RIDING INVISIBLE

written by

SANDRA ALONZO

Illustrated by **NATHAN HUANG**

HYPERION
NEW YORK

For Yancy — Our talented son.

Happy Birthday!

Enjoy your journal.

Love, Dad & Mom

DAY ONE

7PM—AT HOME

I haven't written a thing. Eight months of nothing and it's time to begin, but what should I call this? My Adventure Journal? Everyone has to know the truth in case I get killed on the trail. It'll be My Escape all written and drawn **WHILE IT HAPPENS.** Could be a little raw. I'm a little raw. I've got my flashlight, my pen, the art pencils, and I'm ready to run. My brother, Will, is staying home—good thing. There's no other choice for me.

I'm going to lay low, still and quiet, blend in, harmonize with the world out there. It's not an easy thing to be ▓▓▓▓

—a boy on a HORSE

. . . riding invisible

1

STILL DAY ONE—
10 p.m.—about a half mile from home

Here I am all wrapped in a sleeping bag and it's
weird and scary, and at least it's not all freezing
cold tonight. But I'm out here alone hiding on
this craggy, rocky hill, where the moon shines on
the edge of Chatsworth and the lights remind me
of familiar places. It's like I'm so close but really
far away too. And the moon's hanging there, so
nice like a strange piece of exotic fruit, like it's
wondering who I am, like maybe I'm a starved

my home
CHATSWORTH, CA

wolf. Hey, moon! I'm not starving. Not yet. It's my first night out here. And I'm not going to howl at you either, so forget it.

PLANS

Tomorrow—
guess I'll ride up Mission Blvd. to Foothill Blvd. Then head down to Lake View Terrace. It'll probably take all day and it's a good thing Shy was just shod, with all the pavement his hooves are gonna pound. We have to get out, so we'll disappear fast on the Palmdale trail, which will be a ride of maybe fifty miles to get there, and that might be pretty rough. Or fun. But no one will search for me that far from home. There should be ranches on the outskirts—possibly jobs—a place for Shy???? I don't know. Palmdale could be anything.

Right now—I'm in a cave. No one knows about this place, my hideout, my crawl-inside-and-stay-here place where nobody lives. Shy's hitched out

front chewing weeds—
CHOMP CHOMP—like
a song—**CHOMP**. I left
my iPod home because my
stupid brother borrowed it.
CHOMP! CHOMP! CHOMP!
It's a chewing-weeds song,
so who needs an iPod?

Before one day goes by,
my parents will post signs.
In less than a week, my
photo will decorate milk cartons. I wonder which
photo they'll use? I like the shot Gomez took when
we went skiing and I'm completely out of focus with
that orange knit hat low on my eyebrows.

For sure they already informed the police. I can
imagine that scene:

4

What a bunch of bull. Of course they know why. It's my brother **WILL** who is NOT okay in his mind, like really for sure the guy's completely off his beam, and anyway (whoever finds this and is reading it) the doctors still haven't deciphered what prevents him from being human, but they call it **CONDUCT DISORDER.**

(the reason I may not sleep tonight)

DAY TWO—

early morning—still here in this cave

So it's like I woke up going, Where AM I? Where are my bedroom walls? Then Shy stamped his hoof really hard outside the cave, and I heard the sound and figured it out. Yeah, today's the beginning. The Big Adventure is now.

I can hear this dry Santa Ana wind starting up, and it knocks trees around, steals their leaves. Shy's still eatin' those brownish-colored weeds, which is great because it helps conserve the alfalfa pellets I took from Frank's stable and shoved in a plastic bag.

I do know it's going to be weird riding the 'hood through almost ten miles of middle-class America to reach the north end of the valley and then find that Palmdale trail. It's like this horse (and his four clicking horseshoes) has to haul himself past so much city stuff like hundreds of tract homes displaying their Home Depot landscaping and all these stucco shopping centers and half-empty strip malls. We'll navigate across car-packed boulevards and wait at lights where hopefully the traffic cams avoid us. I'll be wearing a gigantic backpack and riding a loaded-down equine. Now what cop is **NOT** gonna stop that kind of pedestrian?

My big reward for the morning, eaten in five bites—Will's raspberry-jelly doughnut. How he bought it special, all for himself, and left it on the counter even though Dad yells about ants when he does that. And this doughnut tasted like sweet gooey freedom every time I bit into it.

STILL DAY TWO—
probably noon—Mission Park

WHAT I'VE SEEN SO FAR
- jagged graffiti under a bridge made from gang piss in a spray can

- three cop cars surrounding a group
of evil-lookin' gangbangers
and I'm relieved they created their diversion
because I bet those cops
would notice ME and THIS would be over

∘   an old man leaning against a lamppost
his watery red eyes staring
straight into mine
I dug in my pocket for a dollar
and he snagged it like a frog trapping a fly
so I pulled my hand back *FAST*
like I just got bit

From here, the distant mountains look like huge
lavender globs of bubble gum reminding me of that
wad Christi pulled out of her full-lipped mouth to
throw at Bryan, the soccer hero. All the girls at
school say Bryan is just sooooooo hot. Anyway, I
remember how the gum bounced off my knee and
Christi didn't even notice.

A half hour later—still in Mission Park—how stupid
to sit here and WRITE, not keep moving, but I
am addicted to this journal already. Anyway, after
a nice Taco Bell burrito, with mild sauce oozing
out the bottom with every bite, I heard this small
voice on the sidewalk: MIRA, MIRA. CABALLO, MAMÁ. And
even though I don't speak much Spanish, I knew
what this little boy in the blue-flowered stroller
was saying. And his MAMÁ (who looked my age)

8

smiled at me and nodded her head. So I grabbed
the kid under his armpits and put him down real
careful in the saddle. His eyes got Wide-Wide-
Wide, and when I led Shy around the park, my
escape-partner horse totally understood his new
responsibility—I could tell by the way his hooves
moved so slow. The kid went into happy-trance
mode. He couldn't believe how his day just turned
perfect. And when I gave him back to MAMÁ, her
hand brushed against my arm, and anyone could
tell that our skin's the same color. GRACIAS, she
told me, and at least I knew what to say to
that. DE NADA, and then I hoisted my butt into
the saddle and the leather creaked.

STILL DAY TWO—
about 7:30 p.m.—above Hansen Dam

Here for the night in a dry, deserted wash.
Getting to this location really wasn't so terrible.
You'd think horses ride up and down these
boulevards on a regular basis. So now I guess
we're in Little Tujunga Canyon where a few
miles of baked sand and river rocks and skinny

9

bamboo stalks fill the space. Near some houses at the mouth of the canyon, these spindly, forgotten trees filled with pomegranates gave me some fruit. And for a snack, I used Dad's knife, cutting into the leathery husk to eat all the gritty, sweet and sour seeds that stained the tips of my fingers the same color as the Merlot wine Mom drinks. Afterward I rode Shy up the middle of the creek, listening to his hooves splash against the water, each sound blending into the one before it.

Right now, he's tied to a tall oak, eating alfalfa pellets right off the ground, and hopefully no toxic acorns get mixed in. I'm worried he might end up tangled in his rope, which is long enough so he can lie down tonight.

So what's above us on the creek? A sewage treatment plant? HA! I'm wondering about it because I just used my hands as a cup to suck up some water, and I really don't want to catch an incurable intestinal disease. Didn't some hikers die from something awful last year after they drank from a mountain stream??

All the sagebrush hills are sun-torched-scorched, and the wide, flat canyon presses in real close because both sides are squeezed together by bushy hills, sort of like where I live but less spread out. Chatsworth has huge rock formations, but not here. The plants by the creek smell like something. Microwave popcorn? And my nostrils are all dry and nasty. A huge upside-down V of honking geese just flew over, crossing through the sky like a team, making me wish for friends.

A few months ago, Mom and I watched an old black-and-white Western movie. It was so lame with this cowboy on the run from the law, but shit, that guy was prepared! I mean, he wasn't eating pretzels for dinner. He had a campfire and bacon and these hard biscuits and dried beef. And here I am without even matches. Me Urban Cowboy. Yee-haw!

My sleeping bag's spread on these prickly oak leaves and baked yellow grass. What a bed. I will pray tonight that no rattlesnakes or scorpions climb in to sleep with me and that a rabid coyote doesn't drag me away. A bunch of California quail just ran by. Is it a covey of quail? Not a flock. Anyway, they're pretty, with one proud black feather on top of their heads. My mom always says, "Listen to their call. It sounds like they're saying CHI-CA-GO! CHI-CA-GO!"

MY NEW LIFE
IN THE WILD WEST

the last bit of light fades and
my sleeping bag hugs
this horse-scented body
while little brown rabbits
dart in—dart out
the local chaparral is sunburned
and shriveled and branches snap
with creepy sounds

my thoughts vibrate like zinging bullets
so I dig inside the backpack
until I find Dad's knife
I will sleep with it tonight
sharp cold peace of mind
even though there's no way possible
for Big Brother Will to find us here

12

More "back story"—can't sleep—it's those freakin' sounds.

WHAT'S WILL LIKE?

- handsome—girls say he's twisted but cute
- charming—only when he wants something
- smart—never gets A's but could if he wanted to
- sneaky—always manages to not get caught
- bad temper—yeah, and seeks revenge, too
- innocent—it's, like, never his fault

Will's Worst Characteristic:

PHYSICALLY CRUEL
TO PEOPLE (like younger brothers)

AND ANIMALS (like my horse)

DAY THREE—
early—above Hansen Dam

So this morning on the Trail to Wherever,
the fog was a thick, wet, way-heavy WALL,
and I'm sitting here under a rain tree trying to
write on a damp page. I packed my stuff when it
was still dark, and we've ridden for a few hours
already before it gets hot. So maybe I'm starting
to wonder why the hell I'm out here eating
pulverized potato chips and a bruised mushy apple
with a label that says GALA. Now the sticker's
on my cheek where I stuck it because GALA
sounds so fun, like there's this GALA event out
here where it's moist and chilly and where Shy
practically inhales his feed, and I worry when it'll
run out. He keeps giving me these sad-eye stares,

14

and I'm sure in his small horse brain he thinks I've gone nuts.

Horse questions:

1. Dude! Where's the barn?

2. Like, where's my regular hay and how come you're so stingy with these pellets?

3. And not only that, I need water, okay? Where's the freakin' water? Huh??

STILL DAY THREE—
early afternoon—15 miles(?) above Hansen Dam

So by the time we reached a rocky fire road, the little stream was long gone, the canteen was almost empty, and the sun had started to break through cloudy clumps of haze. My palms kept trying to choke the soft leather reins. Shy's gonna colic if he can't drink. That's what horses do. They colic, and I've seen that before, a colicky mare, and it was terrible how she thrashed around and bit at her sides, pawing and sweating, all out of control. They transported her to the equine hospital, operated, and saved her.

"WE NEED WATER!!"

I just yelled it. No one answered.

This horse has heart. He pushed forward all morning, a tireless machine. Finally, he found a trail behind the chaparral where we dropped deep into a shady oak grove. I turned hopeful and Shy did too, because he stamped his front hoof in some oozing mud and then lowered his nose to snort and sniff. Oh, it sucked of disappointment. Sorry, boy. No water. And we stared at the mud, both of us in our separate worlds of wanting and not receiving.

And now while we're resting, while my pen moves across this dry paper, there is nothing to drink. This whole thing is crazy! What was I thinking, doing this on a horse? We should turn around. My common sense tells me, "Go home. Go straight home, dude. Get that horse back in his barn where he wants to be."

But we can't go back. There's a reason why we're out here running. I'm so exhausted, I don't

want to think about it. I'd rather draw Christi
and think about her.

Fantasy Girl

school art club meets on Wednesdays
Christi will be there tomorrow
and me? I am

here
on this lonely trail sitting on my sore butt
and I just ate another meal of mushy apples
and mashed potato chips and
I'm checking out my new warped

life where silky strands
of parasitic plants
grab the chaparral
Hairweed, Mom calls it
reddish-orange like Christi's

hair. I don't know her very well
and she sure as hell doesn't know ME
but sometimes I sketch her with colored
pencils

hair
lemon cadmium #0200
orange chrome #1000
scarlet lake #1200
eyes
mineral green #4500
kingfisher blue #3800
copper brown #6100

personality
a baseball cap tilted to the side
reading glasses nerdy but cute
freckles all over the place
and a tiny little diamond on the nose

and how she always
has something sarcastic to say
and everyone laughs (except for the
teachers)
but out here lost and lonely
I mainly just remember HER

God, I sound like a lovesick dipshit. I must be a
Lovesick Dipshit. Note to self: Perfect title for
romance-less teen novel I should write one day:

Yancy, the Lovesick Dipshit

STILL DAY THREE—
4:30 p.m.?—small clearing—20 miles? from home

The fire road eventually narrowed until it forked off to form a trail, and we were both sweating like horses without even one drop of drinking water in our guts. All of a sudden, this sign on a post seemed to burst out of the ground like a strange, fast-growing tree, and what it said made me swallow hard, my mouth all dry like that time I accidentally took three decongestant capsules instead of one.

⬅ **ARROYO VISTA PARK**
2 MILES

Key word: PARK!! That must mean WATER!! Drinking fountain, right? Maybe a creek. So we turned left. My body sucked in arms and legs as soon as I noticed the first poison oak branch. The red-leaved autumn bushes aren't so toxic right now, but I am way allergic to the stuff, and it bordered the trail for the next two miles.

Two thirsty miles! Shy plodded along and I counted the steps out loud until we finally reached

WATER WATER WATER WATER glorious water!

The horse plunged in up to his knees gulping around the bit, guzzling like a sucking slurping celebration with the magical stuff dribbling off his whiskers, a mini-waterfall. Every time he raised his head it reminded me of a bearded goat in a rain forest downpour. When he wouldn't drink any more I guided him up a hill toward a small park building and dismounted beside the drinking fountain.

MY TURN!

Inside the park headquarters I found a public toilet, used it, then dipped my head in the dirty sink and splashed water on my face. When I walked out I noticed this middle-aged woman behind the counter and wiped my face on my shirt. This lady was wearing her name tag: JOAN, and a khaki shorts uniform. She had all this curly gray hair and white-framed glasses and these awful crooked yellow teeth that I noticed when she smiled at me. On her desk an open bag of peanuts was hanging around, along with a bunch of shells that were all over her work space and on the floor. Oh, and a hot-lookin' novel beside her laptop, probably one of those hopeful sagas written by some other Lovesick Dipshit.

"May I help you?" she said, staring at my cheek.

Oh yeah, the GALA sticker! and I ripped it off and asked in my Good Manners Voice, "Yes, please. Um, where's the Palmdale trail, ma'am?"

JOAN glanced at the wall clock (3:15), and she studied the phone on her desk, scratched her forehead under the khaki hat, her eyes narrowing behind the gigantic frames. "You going there on horseback, young man? To Palmdale?"

And then I realized if she were to suspect how I'm one of those runaway types, for sure she'd report me.

"No way!! I'm not riding to Palmdale, definitely not today. Today I'm just heading home. I live really close to here. But my dad wants to ride his horse to Palmdale someday soon because he heard about the trail."

And so JOAN nodded her head, but her lips tightened into a thin, wrinkled line. She cleared her throat. "The trailhead is a mile down the road past the McKenzie Ranch on the right. Tell your dad to look for the U.S. Forest Service marker when he reaches the turnoff."

I said thanks to her and smiled nicely, and then I backed out the door waving my hand like a bad kid who's leaving the principal's office. Oops! Bumped into the watercooler. Sound effects: sloshing wave smacks cement wall. JOAN shook her head like she had me ALL figured out. **THE KID WITH A FRUIT STICKER ON HIS CHEEK IS ALSO AN AWKWARD IDIOT. JEEZ!**

Shy was resting under a tree. I unhitched him and led him back to the creek so he could drink without the bit this time. He tanked up real good and I put his bridle back on, shoved $ in the vending machine for an orange soda, icy cold. Fizzy! It blasted me straight into a carbonated orange grove, my eyes scrunching with that tickling, bubbling effect in the back of my throat.

And when I rode off into the sunset I figured maybe my new friend, JOAN, might be calling the sheriff inside her dreary boring nothing-to-do-all-day office.

STILL DAY THREE—
6:00 p.m.—on top of some mountain someplace

I know I got JOAN's directions straight . . . but they SUCK! She probably did it on purpose, and now it's getting dark, and maybe if I scream like a two-year-old, that'll help, but hey, no one's listening except for Shy, and he doesn't understand screaming.

My top-of-the-line trail horse found the trail JOAN described, if you can call it that. It's this dirt-bike trail all buried in silver-gray thorny brush that pokes through my jeans, steep enough to make my horse struggle and blow hard through his nostrils. Once we reached the ridge, the trail slanted to the downhill again, then veered back up at an impossible angle. At the top of the mountain I decided there was at least enough space for me to sit, and that's what I'm doing right now.

I'm taking a breather in about four square feet of empty dirt in the middle of an abrasive forest where Shy is eating sage. His chin brushes against the hair on my head when his neck dives to the right, then to the left, a chewing machine, a branch-crushing maniac. His actions produce one of those comforting scents because Mom burns sage when she meditates, creating little smoke signals on the inside of our house. Anyway, the sunset just turned gray, so we'd better get ourselves the hell outta this place.

STILL DAY THREE—
about 7 p.m.—location unknown

So now I'm trapped. If I can just climb out of here tomorrow morning I guess I probably won't die, but this could be my grave.

After we'd rested, I hopped back in the saddle and we went along for maybe 10 minutes until Shy squeezed through a narrow passage in the bushes. In the dim light it looked like the trail had disappeared. So I backed him into a tight keyhole space, and without warning his legs thrashed and he struggled hard, lurching, collapsing with the ledge giving way, falling, tumbling in slow motion.

DOWN DOWN DOWN DOWN DOWN

watch

    me

        fall

So now I am in shock at the bottom of some gully. I tried to stand, but my knees gave out. Probably nothing's broken. The bandanna that was once inside my pocket is now wrapped around my head, because my forehead's bleeding. At least I've got my backpack, and maybe it saved my neck from snapping in half. And I've got my journal and the flashlight, too. I tried yelling HELP! a few times, which is ridiculous. Shy's up there someplace. When I called for him, my scream became an empty echo. No telling where he's at. My mind can picture plenty—ALL BAD. Looks like I'm sleeping here. The sand is soft. For sure I'm alive.

I've got my journal, so if you are reading this, like if you're some person who went hiking and

ran across my body or my skeleton, please call my
parents. The phone number is on the inside of the
front cover. I'm sure Will's gonna celebrate my
death, because he'll get to be an only child, which
is his main wish in life. Tell him I hate his fucking
guts. But maybe there's another alternative:

THE TRUSTY CELL PHONE!!

my thumb presses "pwr,"

and my inner voice says

GIVE UP

that's what I usually do

GIVE UP

let my brother win

GIVE UP

I would but the tiny screen says

NO SIGNAL

No signal? They call it fate. But, hey, no
signal—isn't that another kind of signal, like a
sign? A sign telling me that I'm in charge here.
Me in charge of me. Me in charge of my life.
Literally. Shit! So this is when I should get it
all down. Like, in case I die. If it comes to that.

Horse History:

Five years ago I took a job down the street
mucking out Frank's corrals. After about a
month, inside Stall 4, I discovered my ticket to
temporary freedom.

His registered name, Shy Poco Doc: a gorgeous
buckskin worth $10,000 before the leg injury,
but his cutting days were over. Frank said I could
adopt the horse for free. He showed me how
to make that bowed tendon heal. It took six
months for Shy to get strong, and now he can
go forever.

Most Important Thing: Every minute spent
on the trails is another minute away from my
brother.

Second Most Important Thing: Isn't it weird
how my best friend is a horse?

Third Most Important Thing: Shy, the new horse
I got when I was ten and Will was eleven, made
it even more clear that Will hates my guts. But
no one else seemed to notice.

DAY 3?? DAY 4??—

early morning? late night?—down in the gully

I'll never fall asleep, not stuck in this dark pit. I
vomited and now my mouth tastes like crap while
I practice my own form of meditation:

calm calm calm Yancy just be calm

I don't want the flashlight batteries to go
dead. I can't write forever. Please, God, is Shy
okay? I've been staring into blackness listening
for horse sounds, but all I hear is an owl. My body
is hurting.

So it's back to thoughts about Will. Is
anyone capable of figuring out his warped mind?
Maybe it's related to FREEDOM—who has it—
who wishes they could have it—and what the fuck
is freedom anyway?

That's my opinion. If I get a car before Will, which is probably what will happen, he'll slash my tires and sabotage the engine, and maybe he'll blow the sucker up. It's how his mind works. Payback is everything.

He has to pay me back for not having conduct disorder.

The guy is very smart, way too smart to get caught. Like, even though Will's supposed to be at the YMCA Teen Center every day after school, he can arrange to NOT be there whenever it works for him. The busy counselors never miss Slick Will, Escape Artist of the Century. For sure he'll return before 6:00 p.m., looking all innocent and relaxed when Dad arrives to pick him up.

Anyway. Two days before My Escape and Will was waiting at Shy's corral.

"So, jerk-off," he told me that day. "I need some money. Ya got some cash, little bro?"

He flipped his peroxide-streaked hair over his right shoulder and stepped in close, too close. I could smell Reese's Pieces on his breath. BAM-BAM-BAM, my heart goin' all crazy, and I told myself to make up something in a hurry. So I lied and explained how my money was at Gomez's house.

"Okay, Loser Boy," Will said, motioning toward me with his hand. "Let's go to Gomez's then. C'mon, Fancy Yancy. Move it!"

The Backside IS His Best Side

Will's new underwear
hugged the middle of his butt
above his favorite faded pants
four inches of red boxers
advertising DANGER
as I watched him stride away

YOU'RE NOT GETTING A DIME. NOT THIS TIME. I sprinted past the corral in the other direction. A breeze ruffled Shy's mane, and his awesome tail swung to the side like a grass skirt on a dancing island girl. He snorted and watched me leave.

Behind the stables there's a field packed full of tall weeds and ditches and abandoned cars and furniture. Perfect! I crouched low and waited, noticing how the eucalyptus trees smelled like cough drops. I decided to lie back, enjoy the scent, watch the sky. Will called my name a few thousand times, pissed off, definitely in Manic Mode. But I kept staring at birds. Then I tracked a massive cloud formation blowing in from the west. Finally Will gave up.

After about thirty minutes of silence, I jogged over to groom Shy before going home. The first thing I noticed was something black piled on the dirt, like maybe the wind had blown a dark-colored scarf inside the corral. I opened the gate and a breeze curled around my feet. The black stuff fanned out, and that's when I realized what he'd done.

The Local Psychopath had cut off my horse's tail!! Shy was left with only a stub. Just hair had been cut off, and he wasn't actually harmed, but hey, my horse was robbed.

So I went marching home carrying Shy's tail, and the useless clump of stuff flowed from my fist, a physical thing that displayed Will's evil action; it swept the ground and felt so lifeless in my hands. I dumped it on the dinner table where they were eating macaroni, and the pile of dusty horsehair formed a shape like a question mark. Mom gasped and her green eyes got wide—same color as Will's—and Dad told me: "Get that off the table, son, whatever it is."

I pointed at Will. "Why don't you ask HIM what it is?"

And my good-looking brother smiled with his perfect, could-do-dental-commercials teeth. He put on his fake, exemplary Mom Voice. "Yancy dearest, what have you brought home for dinner tonight? My goodness. It's terribly filthy."

something in me shattered
fragile
breaking like a lightbulb hitting
a tile floor

"Your boy Will's an insane sicko!" I screamed, while my parents stared at me, and Will sat there grinning. "I mean, like, horses NEED their tails. That's how they get flies off their bodies, and fly season's not over for two months. Shy just lost three feet of fly protection, thanks to my stupid brother!"

"Are you saying Will intentionally cut off Shy's tail?" Dad said, or yelled, or whatever, and he jumped out of his chair looking really pissed.

Will jumped up too. "No way! He's a liar!" His voice all confident sounding.

Dad's fork dropped. CLINK! He headed toward Will. It was getting way too intense for an enjoyable macaroni and cheese meal, so I escaped to my room and locked the door, but I could hear them scream. I could hear Will holler, "Not me! You always blame me!" And then a loud crash. I wondered if it was the sound of Dad hitting Will. But Dad isn't supposed to hit Will—that's what he and Mom learned in their Behavior Therapy Class a long time ago, that Dad has to stay calm and firm and give Will positive reinforcement when he does something good. Hey, it's a psychologist-approved behavior program for their out-of-control, majorly insane son.

About fifteen minutes after all the screaming, Dad knocked on my door, but he couldn't get in because it was locked. "Yancy," he called from the hall. "It is not okay for Will to do crap like that. Open the door and let's talk about it."

I turned up the volume on my iPod.

"Yancy!" Dad rattled my doorknob. "You in there?"

"No."

"Okay, fine. Tomorrow we'll talk about this during our family conference."

Thirty minutes after that, Mom's soft tap. "Sweetheart? You didn't eat your dinner. I left a plate on top of the microwave. I think Will feels badly about what he did. Yancy? You okay in there?"

I turned the music up even louder. What were they supposed to do? Put Will in handcuffs? He'd never touched my horse before. Why now? Was this a normal progression of Conduct Disorder Mind Warp? If my favorite thing in the world was a goldfish, would he fry it for dinner?

I needed time to think. My only hope was the stupid Family Problem-Solving Conference, these monthly meetings where we all had to sit in the den, face-to-face, prepared to discuss our family trauma and drama. I usually hated those conferences because they're completely boring and nothing was going to help Will anyway. My parents use the Behavior Therapy Approach, a way-useless tool, IMHO. How come I'm the only one besides Will who knows that? But since we are equal members in this family, I was supposed to have EQUAL POWER, but only if I spoke up at the meetings. But whenever I complained about Will, he made me pay later, and if I complained that he made me pay, then he made me pay for that. It just never ended.

But this time was different. I wanted revenge! All day at Frank's I was thinking, **MY HORSE HAS NO TAIL**. This time it wasn't about me. I would not sit there with my mouth taped shut as usual. I would have to say something about Will's sick behavior.

And that's what I did. As soon as everyone reached the den, I climbed to my feet and blurted it out. "Shy lost his amazing tail and even worse, he's gonna suffer. Will should lose something amazing, too. Something he's proud of, right? My suggestion is that we shave his freakin' head."

Will reached back and stroked his ponytail.

36

"Dude! We are not living in some ancient civilization. This is Chatsworth!"

"Well, what you did was barbaric. A ponytail for a ponytail. It's fair!"

Will glanced around. "Dad! Mom! Tell him his idea is ridiculous!"

Of course they agreed with my brother. Ridiculous with a capital R. So I went with PLAN B, that Will should lose TEN points off his chart toward earning his learner's permit, and Dad and Mom said PERFECT! while Will did some cussing and screaming. They told him the ugly words would cost another point, so he shut up.

Then we squeezed into the bathroom, and they took Will's pathetic little cutout race car that he's got all tacked to some pathetic Microsoft clip art chart. It might work for a six-year-old, but hey, this dude is sixteen, and they made Will take his race car and move it back eleven spaces. So that put him on square seven, poor guy, and he needs a hundred squares of positive actions to reach his goal.

WHAT I WANT by Will Aparicio
I really want to earn a learner's permit so I can drive a car so I can be a famous race car driver when I grow up.

START
FINISH
MY GOAL: DRIVER'S LICENSE

When we left the bathroom, on the way back to the den, Will glided down the hall toward Dad. "So how can I earn some of those points back?" he said so nicely, hanging his arm over my father's shoulder the way guy-pals do. "Can

I wash your car, maybe? That should be worth a point or two."

And Dad said okay! Only one lousy point, but still—fuck! It almost made me puke. The therapists have told my parents, especially Dad, that it is not good for Will to have such a low rate of positive reinforcement, because it's very harmful to his self-image. He needs ample opportunity for success, they say. But here's my POV. On our journey back to the den after the car-busting ceremony in the bathroom, returning to our wondrous Family Problem-Solving Conference, Will flipped me off behind their backs and narrowed his tiger eyes so full of anger and hatred, there was no doubt in my mind about what he was saying:

YOU AND YOUR HORSE
ARE GONNA PAY!!

So it was definite: **WILL AIN'T GONNA CHANGE.** And of course the chilling knowledge: he would find a way to get even. Family Problem-Solving Conferences. Did they help?

I made myself a promise. I would NEVER attend one of those conferences again. I'd have to resolve Will's violence on my own.

God, I should stop writing but the flashlight shines strong with Dad's expensive batteries, and the moon is bright and cheery. Trying to heal me.

And now, down in the gully, I can visualize a hiker finding this journal, buzzards circling my dead body. I visualize the hiker opening my book, looking into what I've written here about my life while he tries to decipher the words and drawings.

WHAT DOES THAT PERSON THINK OF ALL THIS?

Is he skeptical? Does he believe what I've written? Maybe Mr. Hiker is wondering if my parents are negligent. Why haven't they protected me and Shy? If I had a chance to speak to Mr. Hiker, I'd try to convince him how I've been putting up with my brother's shit my entire life. Will's shit is the normal thing. No one seems very worried about me, so I must be fine, right?

Listen, Mr. Hiker. They love me, but they just don't get it. Here's an example:

This one day when I was in the eighth grade, I stayed in bed sick after Mom left for her yoga studio, so she didn't know I was there hanging out in my room when she came home for lunch with a girlfriend.

"How do you stand it, Jessica?" Mom's friend was saying. "Will's a total handful, isn't he? How does Yancy deal with his brother's craziness?"

And Mom replied: "Yancy's okay. He gets A's, he's a good writer, a gifted artist. I think his horse is super . . . you know, a perfect way to escape all the stress around here. Thank God one of the kids is normal."

But, Mr. Hiker, listen to this. Can any brother of Will's be NORMAL? Keep reading. (I've almost reached the violent part.)

The next afternoon, Sunday, the day after the tail incident, he was at the stables again. AGAIN! He was NOT playing softball at the park. *BAM-BAM-BAM*: my heart.

Will laughed and his teeth were so white, and he watched a humongous frantic crow peck at dried horse poop inside Shy's corral.

"So, manure-eater," he told me, "let's go to Gomez's and get that cash."

"NO."

Quick as a slingshot—**SMACK!**—Will's fist

41

slammed against my shoulder, and it made me stumble backward, but I stayed on my feet, left-right-left-right, knees shaking, belly churning. He hit me again. And even though I'd never stood up for myself before, the part of my mind that loves my horse started telling me to fight for the missing tail. I made myself forget that Will is huge and mean and dangerous. Kill Will!!

BAM! My knee landed hard in his groin. God, the stunned look on his face was priceless, like he couldn't believe I'd kneed him, and then he doubled over.

"Fuckhead!" Will staggered into the barn, digging deep inside a tack trunk. He'd really gone crazy, and stuff flew out, and I was ducking and dodging stiff-bristled grooming brushes and a metal currycomb, three rolls of orange vet wrap, a gray bottle of fly spray, and then something shiny and silver waved through the air, but he didn't throw that.

"I've got scissors, asshole, and I'm cuttin' your stupid horse to shreds!" Will leaped inside Shy's corral before I could blink, and his arm lashed against Shy's hindquarters. My horse bolted, all panicked, lunging hard against metal bars, seeking a way out. The animal was trapped. The scissors flashed again, but Shy was dodging the danger. I reached the gate and slid the latch with one fast yank, and it jabbed my thumb, but I was beyond pain. My legs swung up, squeezing Shy's bare back, and he galloped through the gate and bumped into Will, who got knocked to the ground. GOOD! We were speeding, galloping strong, and I had to guide the horse with my knees and we escaped.

"I hope you die!" are the words I screamed.

Of course Will shouted a quick answer: "Your fuckin' horse is gonna die! I'll chop him into little pieces and you'll find his hooves in one place and his ears in . . ."

So maybe when we were about five blocks away I slid off and ran around to Shy's flank. The gash, a thin red stripe, barely a hide wound, not serious. And I was out there without a lead rope or halter or anything, but Shy is well-behaved. He'll follow me anywhere. So my horse buddy and I headed for a place where Will wouldn't find us, behind the concrete wash where the little kids ride their skateboards.

Finally, when I figured Will must be gone, Shy followed me back to his corral. A flake of hay was already waiting inside the feeder, left there by Frank. Then I headed home, feet rising over invisible cracks in the sidewalk, soaring high, but not in an elated way. I kept thinking about what I should do. Should I report what happened? Call 9-1-1? Tell them: "My brother cut my horse with a pair of scissors. The animal doesn't need medical attention, but maybe my brother does. Because I trampled the asshole when I made my horse run him down!" Or should I warn old Frank, the stable owner? His house is pretty far from Shy's corral, so how would he know if Will showed up? There's always Grandma and Gramps. Maybe Shy could live by their pool. And for sure, Mom and Dad are so predictable:

SCENARIO ONE: MOST LIKELY TO HAVE HAPPENED

Will just cut my horse! My suggestion is that you guys post a Rent-a-cop in front of Shy's corral 24/7.

Yancy! Get serious! We can't afford a guard! We'll move Will's race car back one square instead.

Slashing horses?! This is horrible! I think I need to meditate.

Heh heh. There are so many ways to hurt a horse.

By the time I made it home, sweating, all out of breath, I'd already weighed the options. I knew Shy's jagged, shallow cut was an urgent message begging me to freakin' GET OUT!! So instead of telling my parents what happened, instead of doing homework that night, I made a quick list instead.

Shy's Stuff

alfalfa pellets
halter and lead
hoof pick
collapsible bucket
rags
1 roll vet wrap

For Me

backpack   canteen
Dad's knife   toothbrush
food   journal
sleeping bag   art supplies
coat
extra socks and underwear
2 t-shirts and pants

IMPORTANT—my cell phone
and charger

DAY FOUR—
early morning—same location

Now, still stuck in the gully with everything so
hopeless, this mechanical sound just vibrated the
sky like an explosion of thunder:

WHAP-WHAP-WHAP
oh
crap-crap-crap!

   A helicopter. JOAN probably made that call.
They're HERE! And where is Shy? Maybe
he's concealed behind trees or bushes. At least
Shy's the color of what grows on these hills. Or
he could be home, already back in Frank's barn.
Or lost. Trotting around, snorting, not knowing
which way to turn.

WHAP-WHAP-WHAP
the decision hangs over me
like a filthy umbrella

I have to make a choice
and I have to make it now

46

choice #1: remain invisible
choice #2: wave my arms and jump around

The helicopter just made one last pass, circling, whapping its blades, begging me to show myself. But no. I stayed hidden, invisible, clamping my arms against my sides, making myself small, praying I'd disappeared completely under the lonesome weeds.

STILL DAY FOUR—
about 10 a.m.—sitting on a ridge

Listening to that helicopter soar away made me happy and sad all at once, with the sky all blue, so blue—colors can cure injuries—I read that someplace. What if the sky was the color of chocolate? Or raw meat? Or mustard?

The weather right now is humid, sweltering hot. REAL hot. And I'm safe. SORTA safe. And there's this lizard watching me write. I can tell that he used to be a dinosaur, because he's got tiny dinosaur eyes. And he must realize that I'm not dead. Not yet.

Oh, and hey, lizard, guess what? I got myself out of a huge mess. Yeah!

When I climbed out of that wash—for every bit of progress, I always slid down again. Over and over, rocks tumbling, all caving in, my feet barely able to get traction, fingers all bloody and scraped, and tons of prickly bushes on both sides. I decided to toss my backpack to the ledge. In case I didn't make it I figured that someone, like my buddy Mr. Hiker, might find it someday with the journal inside.

Then, the worst. While I balanced on the side of the hill, I grabbed a small bush and the whole freakin' thing came out by the roots, which sent me sliding down about five feet. I tried lunging toward a rock and managed to hang on and pull myself up inch by inch . . . tugging . . . pulling . . . screaming with the effort . . . until finally somehow I got to the top and swung my legs over. Barely.

Right away I heard the bushes crackle in the distance. Shy! Eating grass. Waiting. He whinnied, and the quaking horse-sound engulfed me. I hobbled over, crying and kissed his nose, a big smooch. Then I ran my hands up and down his body—no heat or scratches or swelling. And I walked him out—no limping. The canteen was still hanging off the saddle horn, so I poured what was left into the collapsible bucket. Shy licked the bottom while my tongue sat dry and fat and wanting.

So after I put the bucket away and tightened the cinch and swung my stiff leg over, yelling a little because it hurt so much, I realized that I was back home where I belonged. Back in the saddle.

Shy had to walk slow for me. We rested a lot. After an hour of dead ends, finally we found a decent trail and plodded along for two hours.

No water. Of course no water! Autumn in Southern California equals absolutely NO WATER.

When Shy sweats, the reins foam against his neck. Big drops of sweat fall off his belly. I feel the heat of his body. Our pace, incredibly slow. Our final destination? Freakin' fuzzy.

Did I once call this an ADVENTURE, like it would be some kind of fun...?

STILL DAY FOUR—
about 1:00 p.m.—inside a storage shed

The Five W's:

WHERE? On a small ranch with a peeling-paint yellow house and this wide, sparse yard with a few thorny trees and an old black dog snoozing under a pickup.

WHO? Well, it's me and Shy

WHY? Fuck if I know

WHEN? Today. Tomorrow. Forever!

WHAT? Yeah. That's a good question. Let me ask it again. WHAAAAAAT?

So today, more like about an hour ago, finally we reached **CIVILIZATION**, which means spread-out ranches where the houses are not built close together because they're standing on parcels about two or three acres in size. And the earth here is reddish brown and the plants are dry and the wind is hot and fast. And we're NOT picky. So the first ranch was fine. Just for a break, and maybe some decent horse feed. While a little donkey watched from the next yard over, two ribs-showing horses trotted down a hill like a welcoming committee. Their raspy whinnies made

Shy prick up his ears. He called back and his body shook under my legs.

"You like this place, boy?" I asked my Best Friend the Horse. Then I climbed off the saddle slow and careful, with my calves aching like they'd been stabbed a few hundred times.

The corral was this sagging, rusty barbed-wire creation with dried manure spread around everywhere, and a bunch of gnats, those creepy tiny flies, started irritating Shy's belly. The short stub of a tail twitched, but that didn't help, so he tried kicking his stomach with his hind legs. Someday, to get even, I will tie my naked brother to a tree and smear something all over him, something gnats love...?

When the flimsy gate opened, Shy trotted to the water trough, the inside all green and slimy, murky to the bottom, but he was fine with that and drank deep and big. The two mares squealed and kicked out, and Shy ignored their silliness. And then I shoved my head under the cool rushing faucet with my cracked lips and dried-out skin, and the sores and scrapes burned. It made me realize that maybe I'm a mess. Horse and boy gulped water side by side, me with hands cupped under the faucet, him with whiskery lips sucking against the wet surface. Then I filled the canteen and loved the way it felt so heavy afterward.

With feet moving slow, bones aching, the two exhausted explorers discovered this large metal shed where the door was unlocked. It was full of junk and mouse poop, and I noticed a beat-up broom in the corner. I swept out enough space to sit my butt down and wanted to cry, but I had a horse to take care of. So I struggled to my feet and unsaddled Shy, and the sweat on his light brown coat looked filthy, and jeez, he smelled so bad, and all the flies loved the sweat. Behind the house I found a hose, so Shy got his first bath in four days. He even let me squirt his face, his least favorite place for water, but today he actually twisted his neck toward the gushing stream. And I took a shower too, clothes and all. After that I stole a horse snack, because six bales of grassy alfalfa were sitting on some pallets beside the corral. I broke off a nice big flake for Shy and spread the remaining hay from that bale on the pallets so it wouldn't be missed.

Finally, I settled my hip bone against the non-bouncy cement floor. And just for fun, I started up a short conversation.

"Hey, Mom! What's our snack today?"

"Well, sweetie, the cupboard is almost empty, but here are a few stale cookies. Enjoy!"

STILL DAY FOUR—
about 3 p.m.—school bus stop

Oops—we got evicted from the mouse-poop shed, and that shook me up and brought me here to this covered area beside a dirt road where I'm sitting on a bench in the shade. I got the shit scared outta me in that last place.

After eating the cookies, I curled up in the corner and dozed off. I awoke to a live nightmare because this huge dude with a long blond mustache and a humongous beer gut was all standing there and staring at me, like maybe he thought I was worthless, but at least he was Without Shotgun.

"You speak English, boy?" Mr. Huge Cowboy-Type barked like some kind of official border-patrol canine, like he hated me just for my ethnicity, even though he didn't know my ethnicity.

So I struggled to my feet while I was wishing my skin was lighter, like Mom's and Will's. "Yes, I definitely speak English."

Mr. Cowboy-Type scratched his belly, and it seemed almost funny because I wondered if next he would start scratching his balls. "Well, you're on private property, mister. And that is MY hay your horse is inhaling. Not that you care."

"I do care! We got lost and your shed door wasn't locked. I'm very sorry, sir. We're just taking a break from the sun. I'll give you money for the hay."

"Yeah, well, just get the hell outta here, and I mean right now. Before I call the sheriff!"

It took forever to pick up my stuff and shove it in the saddlebags. I flung the gel pad and Western saddle over Shy's back, and tightened the cinch and breast collar and crupper, all that usual stuff, while that asshole-creep stared me down. When Shy galloped fast toward the gravel-covered driveway, it felt like we were escaping from a weirdo who kills Latino kids for a hobby. It's so wrong. And I wish I could go back home. Now. Tonight. To a place where I have parents.

My mom—English, German, Irish, whatever
  • A mellow person but she panics around
      Will, erases him by meditating
  • What keeps her going: herbal tea,
soothing music, long walks in the hills
      • What she loves: living the life of
          a strict vegetarian, driving a
          hybrid, reading self-help books

Mom's a butterfly

My dad—his father, Latino, born in Arizona,
      his mom from El Salvador
  • An energetic guy, popular with kids, a math
      teacher, funny, strong, good at sports
          makes most of our family decisions
          and keeps Will under control
  • What he loves: tacos and hot sauce,
  Oldies But Goodies, his classic Chevy,
      his Harley, Mom, and his boys

Dad's a hamster on a wheel

I've been watching the sky, and the clouds remind me of being ten years old when Mom, Dad, and I were taking this walk in the hills by our house. I remember feeling a little more bouncy than usual because Will wasn't there. He was on a zoo outing for Kids with Special Needs. The three of us were just walking and having fun, and Mom was teaching me the names of all the native plants and birds. Then Dad started finding funny figures in the clouds:

- dog with a long nose eating a marshmallow
- dragon peeking out of a cave
- deformed heart transmuting into a monster
- (reminding me of Will)

So Dad laughed, and his copper-shaded skin glowed in the sun. "Hey, Yance, look! That one's a chile."

Mom started to giggle like she was a girl in middle school. "Jorge, you always find chiles!"

And I agreed with that. "And you should keep 'em in the sky too, Dad, instead of putting so many in your homemade salsa, because that stuff makes me choke. It's HOT CHILE pollution."

Dad laughed big and happy, and his strong arms circled me, and when I was in the middle of that nice solid hug I made a solid wish . . . that Will would fall in the lion cage and get eaten.

STILL DAY FOUR—
probably 5:00 p.m.—beside a deserted road

I'm a runaway, just a kid who's wondering what my friends learned today in third period geography, being as I'm enrolled in the School of Life on the Road.

GEOGRAPHY:

My idea of geography? It's hot pavement that burns through my jeans while I sit here in the shade of a cactus. It's wondering what's edible for horses in the wild. It's trying to guess how many more miles we've got left to Palmdale. It's asking God where the water's located and how much should horses drink in this kind of heat?

CREATIVE WRITING CLASS:

Destinations

the route we're following
parallels Highway 14
the asphalt twists and climbs
and the earth turns dark orange around
scattered ranches, like scabs
a scorching wind bends bushy pine trees
and Shy's black mane whips over his neck
my stomach growls with emptiness
cars soar by and no one stops
and I just met a man who didn't like me

the things I write sound over the edge
but it's like being in this crazy new world
where I'm the only resident
and the planet is my mind

HEALTH:

Family Studies. Yeah! Assignment: compare and
contrast a functional family with a dysfunctional one.
    Example of a functional family: Gomez and
his big brother, Ramón. Gomez and Ramón
actually hang together and go to parties even.
His brother has a car and drives us places, like to

the movies and the mall, and once he took us
to the beach.

Example of a dysfunctional family: Will
and Yancy Aparicio. My brother is no role
model. Gomez and I try to avoid my house
unless we're sure Will is not around.

GRAPHIC ARTS:

Assignment: Draw scenes that show a good
day gone bad.

PHYSICAL EDUCATION:

Cross-Country Equestrian Olympics! Whoa,
this course almost ended in disaster less
than an hour ago. Our dirt road disappeared.
We actually had to ride up the onramp and

alongside the freeway. Just for two exits, but still. I mean, the whole time I was praying a truck wouldn't run us down. Or what if the Highway Patrol spotted us? But hey, Shy did good. He won the blue ribbon for Most Dependable Mount because he did not even flinch when the big rigs zoomed by.

ALGEBRA:

I wish I could solve the following equation:

$$\frac{X \text{ (me and my immeasurable, one-sided lust)} + Y \text{ (Christi)}}{??? \text{ (dunno, it's freakin' vague)}}$$

What's missing in this unbalanced equation?

BIOLOGY:

Will's heart. God forgot something. It's empty!! A void, a black hole of nothingness.

WILL'S
HEART

60

STILL DAY FOUR—
about 9 p.m.—small park in Palmdale

So for the moment I'm safe, the park is weird, but I'm here and this is what went down earlier:

A sign around 6:00 p.m.:

It made me whoop, **YEAH!!**

   The sound of my yell caused Shy to spook. "Hey boy, it's okay. It's only me, happy me!"
   When we finally arrived in Palmdale, I was so tired there was no energy left for expressing joy. "We're here . . . whoopee." I dismounted and led my horse down a sidewalk, and he walked with his head low and his ears sort of spread out, not alert, not careful. We both filled our water tanks at an Arco, and I asked a little kid to hold the reins for a dollar while I used the restroom

and bought snacks in the mini-mart. Across the street I noticed an IHOP. I led Shy to it and hitched him to the lamppost by the parking lot, bought a local newspaper, stretched my body across the moist grass, ate two hot dogs in about two bites or less, opened a bag of pretzels, and ripped the top off an orange soda. And a bunch of people stared at me. I didn't care. *GO AHEAD AND LOOK! JUST DON'T COME TOO CLOSE BECAUSE I STINK.*

In the want ads, most of the jobs were out of my league. I'm no dental assistant or X-ray tech or whatever. My list of possible leads:

1. nanny for preschool kids
2. construction worker
3. newspaper delivery person
4. field hand
5. tractor operator
6. landscaper

And when I got my cell phone switched on, the battery was low—I brought the charger, but . . . anyway, the little screen announced that there were messages. I couldn't think about it, because probably the mailbox was full of desperate parental calls, and that thought dug at me and poked its skinny arms in my ribs, and still I was able to ignore it and not FEEL what it means to have people looking everywhere to find me. At least I'd disabled the text message alarm and didn't have to listen to the sound.

After dialing the #1 choice from the ads, a woman answered. I explained how I was calling for the live-in nanny position and how I really love kids and my dad's a teacher, etc. And I lied about my age. She said fine, that I should drop by and fill out an application. So then I described the pet complication and she busted up and called to her husband, "Hey Joe, I gotta kid on the line who wants to keep a horse in his room! HA!"

So next I phoned about the construction job:
"You're going to need references."

Newspaper delivery:
"Sorry, it's been filled."

Field hand (a recording in Spanish and English):
"You will need proper identification
proving that you are a legal resident,

or don't bother coming in."

Tractor operator:
"You gotta heavy-equipment operator's license?"

I even tried the landscape number:
"Yeah, we're hiring, but you need
your own truck, plus tools."

About then I tossed the want ads in the
trash and pulled out my wallet: $19.52. Shy's
feed almost gone, two half-digested hot dogs in
my belly. How and where could I buy a fake I.D.
for under $20? And since when do I have to
prove I'm here legally?

So this was how it was going to be. This was
it, the true stuff, life on the road and all that.
After a while I fell asleep on the grass, probably
resembling a dead dog, and when I woke up it was
freezing and I wondered how come it was dark.

And then I spotted this man leaning against
a gray-used-to-be-blue truck in the IHOP parking
lot. Just WATCHING. Which made my heart
stop. And I wanted to look away, but there was
something curious about this guy and his muddy

cowboy boots and his slightly crooked cowboy hat and his dark complexion about my dad's shade, but this dude had a heavier build than Dad.

So he was Latino-looking, thirty-something, and he started coming my way. The man approached slowly and ran his hand down Shy's rump. He examined the butchered tail and frowned at the healing slash, and kind of rested his palm against the wound. So I started wondering what I should do. I mean, shouldn't he ask permission before laying his hands on my horse? But I figured maybe if I could keep my mouth shut and pretend to be invisible, he'd just go away.

But then he started talking. "Nice animal," he said with a heavy Spanish accent, nodding his head in Shy's direction.

His eyes, light brown, gentle—I liked those eyes. Then he wanted to know why I was riding a horse through the middle of a city. Good question, I thought, and shrugged my shoulders and untied Shy's lead from the lamppost, acting all casual and slow moving about leaving. But the man didn't give up, and he walked a few steps to the lamppost and held out his right hand for me to

shake. His knuckles were all scraped, and I studied
his hands and they were working hands, calloused,
and he told me his name. Gustavo Mendoza. Tavo.
He used to live in Mexico.

Get outta here, Yancy, I said to myself. So
I slid the bit in Shy's mouth, and it banged
against his teeth, because by that time I was in a
hurry, and I tucked his forelock under the leather
brow band on the bridle and lifted the reins
over his head and took hold of the crest on his
muscular neck, while I stuck my left foot in the
stirrup to hoist myself up.

"Wait!" Gustavo Mendoza called, and I
detected this sharpness behind his voice at the
back of his throat. And at the same time my
thighs squeezed my horse's barrel, the Gustavo
guy hurried over to his beat-up truck, opened the
door, scrawled something on a napkin, and rushed
over to hand it to me.

"This is my number," he said. "You need help,
MUCHACHO? Call Tavo, okay?"

   I reached for the wrinkled paper
   And shoved it deep in my pocket

Shy's hooves played a tune on the pavement

RUNYANCYRUNYANCYRUNYANCYRUN

Tavo's voice echoed against my back:

"I have a nice warm barn
and plenty hay for that pretty horse!"

RUNYANCYRUNYANCYRUNYANCYRUN

So I rode and I rode, wondering where we could spend the night. When Shy plodded down the crowded boulevards, I wished he was wearing Frank's fluorescent equine leg wraps that glow in the dark for night riding, but they're back in the barn. My eyes scanned the sidewalks when we cruised along and Shy's metal horseshoes pounded rhythms:

WHEREAREWEGOINGGOINGGOING?
WHATAREWEDOINGDOINGDOING?

We reached a busy corner and waited for the light to turn green. This burly girl with tattoos

67

stepped off the curb. Her olive green T-shirt
declared **WAR IS NOT THE ANSWER!** which is a
pretty cool statement, in my opinion. "Can I ride
him?" she asked, and her braces took over her
mouth when she grinned, but just then the light
changed, so Shy and I kept on heading forward.
Just forward. Keep on keepin' on.

walls full of graffiti
cars, trucks, buses,
groups of people

EVERYONE HAS SOMEPLACE TO GO

what are my parents doing right now
is Mom crying nonstop
is Dad ranting and hollering

what is Christi doing right now
I don't have her number
what's the point in calling anyway

So after maybe fifteen minutes of sidewalk
riding we passed this tavern where a pregnant
lady leaned against a large, shiny sign with big

letters printed in this very cool font:

MUST Be 21 yeArs Of AGe Or OLDeR TO enTeR

Her sobs jabbed the chilly night, and the sound made me shiver.

So then finally, around 8 p.m., we got off the busy street and rode through a quiet neighborhood where all these run-down houses filled the sides of the streets and eventually we came to a run-down park.

That's where we are right now, the place where I am writing, me perched on top of a carved-up picnic table like I own it. The brown grass reminds me of rusty nails sprouting like a spiked metal carpet, and tall streetlamps are perfect for suicidal moths, but I don't like to watch them die.

Shy slurped up a bunch of water, and he's been unsaddled. Steam is drifting into the moist air straight off his wet, sweaty coat. God, these are the last of his pellets, and horses eat so much. They can't live on the vitamin-drained, dried-out grass that grows along the roadsides.

In between writing I've been talking to Shy, trying to project a hopeful sound in my voice, even though I know I am trembling in my gut. "Don't worry, boy," I tell him. "There's gotta be a way out of this. You have to trust me, is all." And I leave out the parts about how I don't trust myself, and there's no more feed for either of us, and . . .

Shit! Someone's coming. . . .

STILL DAY FOUR—
11:30 p.m. or later—Homeless City, U.S.A.

Later . . . much later . . . God, a horrible interruption after my last entry and this is why I'm spending the night *HERE*, in this place I've named Homeless City, U.S.A., where all residents remain *INVISIBLE.*

I am keeping the info current and I am not being a Drama Queen when I write that this entry could be my last.

Back in the park I was writing in my journal when a loud, threatening voice made me jump to my feet with my fists raised.

And the voice, gravel-rough-mean: "Hand over your cash, homeboy."

There goes my stomach—big dive—leaves body through asshole, because I figured I was dead. These two guys were big, bigger than Will, and maybe seventeen or older and wearing black knit caps and Raiders jackets. They had plenty of piercings with silver rings on their lower lips and more rings on their eyebrows and studs on their earlobes. Christi might say they gleamed with tacky bling.

"Hand it over," the heavier one ordered. "The wallet! Where is the wallet?"

His eyelashes were white. Both dudes had their legs spread, wearing foul expressions that transformed their faces into masks. Oh yeah, they were ready for Halloween, which happens to be this month, but I decided not to tell them. I also didn't tell them how the yellowish street lighting made them look like corpses. My butt pressed against the picnic table while my mind did nothing—nothing!!

"Give us your cash NOW, or we'll take your horse!" White Eyelashes yelled.

He snatched the air in Shy's direction, which

made Shy toss his head, and I could see that white rim around the top part of his eyes. Fear.

OKAY, I'M LISTENING! And I dug deep in my back pocket and held out my wallet, and the white-eyelashes guy opened it and pulled out all the bills and tossed the wallet on the grass.

"Keep the change!" he screamed. Then, like slimy jerk-offs, they danced through the park laughing and hooting, like maybe they were wild animals, and then they huddled under a lamp to count the loot.

"Shit!" one of them said in the distance. "Hardly worth the effort, bro."

And they kept going, and my energy was zapped, the same feeling as running all the bases when the catcher tags me at home plate. Over! Ruined! (No one cheered.)

I don't remember packing my stuff, but when I hopped in the saddle using the picnic table, I do remember how Shy bolted forward. I do remember his indecision, like he was asking: Left? Right? Straight ahead? Give me some guidance. At least a hint! You, rider. Me, transportation.

And then we disappeared in the darkness, both ambivalent, hesitant, completely zoned out,

riding invisible

Maybe a half mile down the road by some tracks we found this place where I'm hanging right now. Homeless City. We moved in. So that's it and now I'm all scrunched up like a discarded newspaper

inside my sleeping bag cocoon
where I watch the soft orange moon
maybe I'll arrive real soon
buried in this deep, dark gloom
writing in rhyme makes me swoon

And all these guys, hidden in the shadows, high on meth or whatever and talkin' soooo weird.

"Hey, baby," this one person just mumbled with a Southern drawl. "You got some tricks?"

And I wondered, *WHAT IF HE'S TALKING TO ME?*

But, thank God, another person answered in a high-pitched voice, maybe a female impersonator. "Why you be askin', Big Ben? I know you ain't got no money for no tricks from me, sweetheart."

I'm trying to write while I've got Shy's lead rope pressed against my chest, because there's no place to tie him, and anyway I am not separating myself from my horse. I AM NOT STUPID. Shy is standing over me like a protective dog, but equines are about as protective as cats. If they could talk, they'd say, "Sure, go ahead and kill my owner, but don't forget to feed me before you leave."

Every time I poke my head out from underneath my flannel-lined sleeping bag, the air smells like old winos and burnt rubber. At least I have the almost round lunar ball to keep me company, and it rises slow over a telephone pole, and when it finally rests on the "T," I want to close my eyes and coast, stay awake, don't sleep, you have to be on guard, don't sleep, not tonight. I wish I could keep writing all nite long....

DAY FIVE—
morning—near the tracks

I'm still alive. I now measure my success in terms of survival:

74

ALIVE? YAY! DEAD? BOO!

So back to when I was in Homeless City, U.S.A., I did float off to sleep, kind of, squeezing the reins in my fists. And then in the early morning, campfire smoke woke me and also this creaking, rattling noise close to my head. A filthy man dressed in a ripped black parka stared down at me, his arm resting on a blue plastic shopping cart with crooked, wobbly wheels, his shoes totally falling apart and holes in his socks, too. He looked like he hadn't shaved in a while. The air around him smelled like rancid liquor and flat beer.

I rubbed my eyes and climbed to my feet, and Shy poked his nose inside the cart to investigate. Empty aluminum cans and wine bottles banged together, clinking hopelessly against a dusty vase filled with plastic flowers, a pair of cowboy boots, a charred frying pan, and a blow dryer.

"Nice gelding," the cart owner said. Then he checked out Shy's tail. "Well, would y' look at that tail! They always bobbed the draft horse tails when I was a kid, you know. Said it was safer, so the long hair wouldn't get caught in the machinery when the horses pulled the plow. Is this a farm horse?"

"No. He's a trail horse."

The man squinted and his eyes wrinkled shut, and I wondered what color they were. His skin looked like the bark on a tree.

"I used to own a horse when I lived in Echo Park," the shopping cart owner told me. "She was my polo pony. Real, real nice. I mean it. And she was kinda pricey, but I used to be a rich lawyer, mind you, and I had her boarded at the Los Angeles Equestrian Center." The man surveyed my gear and rubbed Shy's nose. "We're all runnin' away, I suppose. And guess what? I have a present for you." He dug deep in his cart and lifted out a smashed box of crackers like it was a fragile treasure and handed it to me and then pointed parallel to the tracks. "There's an empty lot fulla weeds about two blocks down where you can graze the pretty horse."

I ate a few crackers, and they were super tasty, and I thanked the guy and carefully placed the box back in the cart because I was thinking that he needed food more than I did. And I automatically reached for my wallet to give him

76

a couple of dollars. But, oh yeah! I had that bad dream about two losers who sucked up the rest of my limited spending cash, even though they only got $19.

"So hang in there," I said.

"Best of luck to you, boy. You're a real good kid. I can tell that much by just lookin' at you."

A few minutes later, Shy trotted off, me barely balanced in the saddle, my shoulders all hunched like those old cowboy dudes after a gunshot wound, until we arrived at this place I'll call Desperation Junction. And Desperation Junction was a frame of mind with me almost not caring what happened next. At least Homeless City was behind us, with not much up ahead in My Immediate Future.

Shy continued trotting beside the tracks until we found that empty lot the old guy from Homeless City had described. Trash and junk all over the place. Weeds full of burrs and stickers. So, still playing the role of an old cowboy who realizes he's defeated, I slid off the saddle, a sloppy dismount, hitting the ground too hard, which stung the bottoms of my feet. Shy didn't rub his face against my back like usual. If horses can go into Depressed Mode, he was probably in that zone with me. He grabbed at a dead weed, making seeds spray in all directions, and I pulled his head up because I didn't want burrs getting stuck to his tongue.

"Who's that?" someone said, and I glanced behind me. To the left of the tracks, this abandoned building sitting there, no paint, no doors, and all of a sudden two dirty kids appeared in the doorway. They waved. Maybe they were twelve years old.

"Boy, you got some food?" one asked.

I noticed his ripped yellow shirt and dark streaks across his cheeks. The other kid looked cleaner, but with stringy red hair and thin shoulders, his bones pressing against his tattered hoodie. That one stretched both hands toward me. His dark eyes looked almost empty, and I could tell there was a reflection of ME in them. Me and my homeless future.

"Sorry," I said. "No food and no money."

So the red-haired one flipped me off. "Liar!"

And they darted back inside their building. Shy tried to get another bite of those nasty plants, and he stamped his hoof, impatient, hungry. We were both so desperate, starving like those two boys, and that's when I pulled the wadded napkin out of my pocket. The printing, all childlike and the phone number with dashes in weird places, like phone numbers people write in foreign countries.

I led my horse along the tracks for about a hundred yards until we reached an area where there were no weeds with stickers for him to grab, and I didn't even sit down. I figured that maybe the batteries were completely gone on my phone, but one bar remained on the screen, so I dialed, and that's why I'm here writing in my journal waiting for my transient past to catch up with me. I call this place my Town of Defeat.

STILL DAY FIVE—
10:15 p.m.—about 20 miles outside Palmdale

After so much has happened, maybe I'm safe but not for sure. Safety is one of those weird words that for some people are meaningless. I know this because when I was born, Will was already there.

Two hours after I made the phone call, the Mexican Tavo drove up in his faded pickup, and the truck looked especially shabby, because it was hauling this brand-new shiny white horse trailer with the words CIRCLE R. ARABIANS on the side.

"That horse is thirsty," Tavo said. It wasn't a question. He opened a side door on the trailer and reached into the tack compartment, grabbed a blue bucket, and rotated a spigot at the bottom of a small water tank in the corner. Thirty seconds later Shy plunged his nose in the water and guzzled most of what was there.

Tavo helped me pull off the saddle and swung the wide trailer door open in the back. Shy hopped in and I bet he was happy, because there was a flake of fresh hay stuffed in the feeder. When I heard him bite off a big mouthful, I felt better than if someone had just handed me a hamburger. Before Tavo locked the trailer gate, I stroked Shy's short tail.

The man patted my shoulder. "You hungry, son? I pay for DESAYUNO, for breakfast."

Hungry? I nodded my head up and down fast, realizing that this wasn't hunger, this was beyond hunger, and my mouth started to water just thinking about food. Tavo took big, energetic strides heading down the street and I almost trotted like a horse to keep up with him, but what I felt like was a calf heading straight to the slaughterhouse.

Denny's Self-Examination
when I pushed through
the restaurant doors
stepping inside
smelling the sweet
scent of
   FOOD!
everyone gawked
mouths opened
someone laughed
I hurried into
the men's room
checked the mirror
and this is what I saw:

So pretty much like an emotionless robot, after cleaning up the best I could, I pushed against the bathroom door and walked in a not-so-confident way toward our booth. My jeans slid

81

across from Tavo on a blotchy red plastic seat, his hair all matted and flat where the hat used to be. For me, sitting there, watching him study me, felt like being on some weird reality TV show where I HAD to win. If I didn't win? I'd be back in Homeless City.

Tavo frowned and his dark eyebrows pressed together like two fuzzy black caterpillars. "What is your name, son?"

It seems pretty stupid writing about it now, but I didn't want to answer, because even though I had to trust this guy, my Last Chance Person, I couldn't do it. Then my stomach growled. Probably everyone heard, and the maddening aroma of Denny's food invaded my brain until I wondered if maybe I'd pass out.

Tavo asked again. About my name. "You can trust me, son."

So I didn't even lie. "Yancy Aparicio." I gave it up. Just like that.

Tavo nodded and looked at me with an eye-to-eye stare. "Okay, Yancy Aparicio, what you want for eat?"

He grinned and I tried to smile back, but my lips were way too cracked. I almost told the waitress to hurry. *RUN, LADY! I HAVEN'T HAD ANYTHING NUTRITIOUS FOR HOW MANY DAYS? SCAMPER BACK HERE WITH MY PLATE!* And when she set the food in front of me, the smell of it made me kinda dizzy, and it was, like, the best I'd ever eaten, like, ever in my life, even though I usually don't love Denny's, but I did today.

> ham and bacon
> two eggs over easy
> hash browns
> biscuits and gravy
> big glass of juice
> big glass of cold milk

Tavo shook his head and laughed this big belly laugh. "Good food, no?"

I couldn't answer because my mouth was full, so I nodded my head.

He laughed again. "Where you live, son?"

And I studied the black crud under my fingernails. This seemed like a way personal question, no? Where do I LIVE? Do I LIVE anyplace?

Tavo sighed. "You want my help, Yancy Aparicio?"

I kept eating, but I was watching him from between bites.

"You tell me why you are out here alone with that pretty horse. I no want to call the POLICIA, okay?"

¡POLICIA! I knew that word. So I said, "I'm from the San Fernando Valley. From Chatsworth."

Tavo let out a soft whistle. "So far? And why you run away, MUCHACHO? You are so young. How old? Only fourteen maybe."

So I told him I'm fifteen, getting close to sixteen.

Tavo shook his head. "Why you run away? The parents, they hit you?"

"No! My parents would never hit me. It's my brother. I'm running away from him. He's completely wacko."

And then Tavo frowned, like he was trying to translate this part of the conversation. "Wacko?" he asked. "What means wacko?"

All these scenes darted inside my head like a thousand lizards escaping from a reptile zoo. And it's like a movie flashed through me, and I could see so many situations that fit perfectly like the last piece in a complicated jigsaw puzzle. Wacko, wacko, wacko. How to explain it? No one ever gets it. Will is just plain wacko! It would be so much easier to lie and say that my dad's an alcoholic, because alcoholism is an illness folks can relate to. But explaining that my brother's crazy? Wacko?? Even though Will totally defines the condition, because he is the wackiest of the wacko, and you'd better look out if you cross his path, dude, because Will is way wacko. He is so wacko that he might kill a horse and maybe wacko enough to kill me, too.

But Tavo had to believe me, so which Will story should I choose?

Finally the mind movies stopped and I took a deep breath and asked, "Did you see my horse's tail?"

"Sí, the horse, he have a very short tail."

"Right. And did you notice that wound across his hindquarters?"

Tavo said yeah he noticed.

"Well, first my brother chopped off my horse's tail. Then he slashed him with a pair of scissors. Two violent acts, all because I wouldn't give him

85

any money. Maybe he was gonna buy drugs . . . who knows? My parents don't think he does drugs, but I'm pretty sure that's the situation. Even though he's got plenty of drugs they **MAKE** him take. You know, legal drugs. But he must want the other ones, too."

Then Tavo wanted to know Will's age. So I told him. "He's, like, one year older than me."

Tavo stared, sipped his coffee, shook his head.

"It's conduct disorder," I mumbled, my voice coming out all unsure and not strong, because if Tavo couldn't comprehend wacko, how was he going to grasp the technical terms? "It's this mental condition," I said, "and it's very hard to explain, but they've done studies, and his brain chemistry, well, it's actually different from a normal person's brain."

"NO. NO ENTIENDO." The black eyebrows pressed together and I figured he'd be calling the POLICIA any second.

I gave it another lame try. "So you've probably never heard of neurotransmitters."

And Tavo whistled softly at that word, and the bewilderment on his face looked major.

"Well, forget it then."

86

And the tears crept slowly upward and reached my chest, but I held them back, squeezed them inside my nose . . . *PLEASE, GOD, DON'T LET THE FLOOD START NOW.*

And then the restaurant racket took over with kids laughing in the booth behind us, and silverware clinking loud, like a disorganized metal band, and Tavo leaned across the table, and I thought maybe he was going to touch me on the forearm, but he folded his hands and stared at me instead.

"PUES, you have this LOCO brother and he is so bad you ride fifty miles on the back of a horse for escape him?"

OH, JEEZ, LET ME STAY ON THIS REALITY SHOW . . . PLEASE DON'T VOTE ME OFF. "Well, he's scary, believe me," I said, trying to sound convincing and forceful while the movies in my head rotated in crazy motion. "Listen. I'll tell you a story. I have a bunch of them."

I scanned my collection, flip flip, and again, flip flip flip—paused—considered that one, and began.

"When Will was thirteen years old my

parents were losing it because he got violent with his history teacher."

"Your brother, he *HIT* a teacher?"

"Yeah. Miss McDonald. He knocked her over when she tried to break up a fight between Will and these two other guys. After that, my parents tried sending him away to live at boarding school. But within thirty days he'd set the dormitory drapes on fire, so they kicked him out. And that was the best month of my life, the only time we've all been happy, just me and Dad and Mom. The three of us were like, well . . . we were a normal family. You can't imagine what it's like living with my brother. He's a human vacuum cleaner. He actually sucks up everyone's energy. Mom's, Dad's, mine . . . until the only thing left is HIM."

Tavo digested my words, took them in. "There is no energy for you."

"No. None at all. My parents are great people and they're proud of me. But hey, they're just relieved I'm not out doing bad things all the time. That way they can focus on Will, because he *IS* doing bad things."

Tavo's face distorted into this disbelieving

expression. "And your parents. They *LET* your brother do these bad things?"

"No! Of course they don't let him. But Will is like a runaway train charging down the track, out of control, unstoppable. Plus there's a lot of stuff they don't even know about, believe me. That's because I keep my mouth shut."

"You no tell the parents what he do?"

"Not usually. It's a waste of time. I did tell them when Will cut off my horse's tail, but nothing much came of it. So the next day when he used scissors to slash him, I figured, why even bother? And then I ran away."

Tavo's expression was telling me that he just didn't get it. I felt like jumping on top of our table and shouting: *HELP! IF YOU UNDERSTAND CONDUCT DISORDER, PLEASE RAISE YOUR HAND AND EXPLAIN IT TO THIS GUY!*

But I didn't do that. Instead, I remembered the worst thing Will had ever done.

"Okay," I said, "so here's what happened when we were at my Aunt Lila's house a few months ago. It's a perfect example. A horrible, awful example."

Tavo sipped his coffee and waited. I took a

deep breath, gulped down some milk, and tried
to get my thoughts together. "It happened when
Will was wrestling with Burrito, my Aunt
Lila's dog, a Chihuahua, really cute and tiny.
Burrito's teeth scraped my brother's hand. It was
an accident! Not serious at all, but Will's got a
temper, see. He was born angry. He's got mental
problems, like I already said, and anyway, he
threw Burrito against a wall, and the little dog
died. No one was around but me to see how it
happened. Just me. And then Will cried all these
huge fake tears and told everyone in such
a sincere voice, sounding all brokenhearted and
apologetic, how it was an accident. 'I didn't
mean to!' he yelled over and over, so everyone
gathered around, and I decided to keep my mouth
shut. Will is that convincing, and by then he had
me believing it really was an accident. And now
he's been messing with my horse. He . . ." I
stopped and covered my face with my hands.
"He could kill my horse."

    my voice cracked
    the way my lips are cracked because
    it scared me shitless to say it out loud:

he could kill my horse.

HE COULD KILL MY HORSE!!

what kind of person
might comprehend something like that?
maybe this Mexican guy . . . maybe so
because
when I glanced at his face
right away
I knew
this dude is gonna help

I wanted to hug him even though he was a
stranger, but before I could get carried away,
Tavo said, "Follow me."

He left money on the table, and then we
walked outside to the truck and trailer, and he
insisted I call my parents. But if I talked to
them I knew my weak interior would crumble.
So I scrolled through the cell phone contacts
and called our next-door neighbors instead. It
rang—voice mail picked up—*PLEASE LEAVE A
MESSAGE AFTER THE BEEP.*

"Hey, Tim and Eileen, this is Yancy Aparicio.

Would you mind explaining to my folks that I'm okay? And tell them I can't come home, and please ask them to stop leaving messages. I am not listening to any messages and . . . also . . . if you'd let them know . . ."

BEEPING . . . screen flashing . . .
low battery

"tellthemIlovethem."

I shook the phone
wrist snapping
elbow jerking
like I wanted to bring it back from the
dead

We climbed in the truck and Tavo turned the key. His key chain dangled, a plastic emblem with red, white, and green letters, M-E-X-I-C-O spelled out in the center. The engine sputtered, and his truck kind of danced down the street while we bounced like two crazy rubber balls almost in rhythm to the emotional Mexican music that wailed on the radio. Ol' Tavo tossed his head back and belted out lyrics, acting carefree like everything was going his way, but I wasn't so positive that everything was going MY way. I was thinking how this Mexican cowboy could be a really great actor. Like maybe he had plans to get rid of me. Dump my body out in the desert. Would he torture me first? Then he'd sell Shy for a whole lot of money. For one thing, where did he get the fancy horse trailer? Something wasn't making sense.

But then I realized how maybe he was genuinely a good person, because he stopped at Long's Drugs and hurried inside and then tossed a bag at me when he returned. Medicated lip balm. The expensive kind, so I put a bunch on my lips, and after that I could actually smile.

Miles later, overflowing with Mexican music, surrounded by empty sand and scraggly sage, we reached our destination and drove under a big, carved wood sign:

TRIPLE R ARABIAN FARM
Home of world class stallion
AL MARAH LOTHARIO

I was, like, speechless—what could I say other than: "Tavo . . . you **OWN** this place?"

And he started laughing, a big hard internal rumble with tears sliding down his cheeks. "Ay, Yancy. No! Ha! I no own nothing! Me? I am the worker, the hired help around here, the guy who do all the work! Ha!"

And then I was laughing too.

DAY SIX—
12:15 p.m.—Triple R Ranch—in the barn

When Tavo drove under that big sign yesterday, it was obvious that this ranch is a first-class private equestrian center. I mean, irrigated pastures? White-rail-PVC fencing? Two fancy barns? A covered arena with lights? There's even warm water at the wash racks for pampered horse bathers. Frank would die to see this place.

Tavo and I bounced along in his rattle box of a truck, and I stared while the driveway sloped up a hill until, all of a sudden, I was Jack at the top of the beanstalk, looking straight at a mansion glaring white and elegant like an uprooted house from Beverly Hills, almost like it was floating up there in the dark gray sky.

Around the back of the barn, we unloaded Shy and took him straight to a clean stall. Inside, the floor was all covered with thick rubber mats and fluffy, sweet-smelling pine shavings. Tavo piled hay in the feeder, but Shy charged past the hay, lunging toward the corner where he pushed his nose against the automatic waterer. I listened to it gush, soothing, like I was inside a spa where worries aren't allowed.

Then we unloaded the trailer, and Tavo tossed my gear at me. "You need a shower before you meet SEÑOR Arnold," he said. "We gonna tell the boss that you my nephew from San Diego, okay?"

And I said sure okay while I was thinking, **YEAH, I WILL LIE. I WILL DO ANYTHING BECAUSE SHY HAS FEED AND PLENTY OF WATER.**

"You bring clean clothes?" Tavo asked, and I told him uh-huh, still in the saddlebags. So Tavo led me to a travel trailer with four inches of gravel out front covered by pale yellow-and-brown leaves and two bare trees standing tall and sad.

I kept moving while my feet shuffled through
the leaves, and through slender branches that
had fallen on the ground, so dry and so brittle,
crackling **CRUNCH-CRUNCH** under my boots,
CRUNCH like the sound of a cat eating a bird.

Singing in the Shower

how long has it been since I had one?
in the very compact trailer
the miniature shower
contains a tiny nozzle
and the spray made me feel
like I was baptizing myself
> reborn!
> clean!
> new!

water streamed
in warm sheets
filling the white square floor
with dirt
my dirt
and I almost felt safe
inside the confined space

but Will's image rose in the steam
I could feel his laughter circling
circling
seeking me out telling me:
DON'T GET TOO HAPPY, DUDE
YOU'LL NEVER SHAKE ME LOOSE

he rode the vapor
like a vulture
scouring the highway for
roadkill

I swept my hand
through the moist hot air
to erase
Will the Vulture
and doing that
made me sing

So after my amazing, unbelievable, super-
fabulous shower with WARM water and IVORY
SOAP, it was time to meet the owner of the
Triple R. Tavo and I climbed the driveway by
the front of the big house where Mr. Arnold was

waiting to meet me, standing beside a fantastic bronze statue of a galloping Arabian horse. And for sure this guy looked like a designer cowboy. (I bet he never gets on a horse.) The outfit included a leather jacket with long fringe, brand-new stone-washed jeans, a gourmet cigarette, and an expensive Western hat. Oh, and snakeskin boots. Plus—the best detail of all—not one molecule of dust anywhere.

Before we shook hands, the boss moved the unfiltered cigarette to his left hand. "Nice to meet you, Yancy," he said with a hint of a European accent. "Tavo explained that you're visiting for a while. How interesting to discover he has relatives in the States." Mr. Arnold turned toward his employee. "I never knew you had people here."

And Tavo grinned, stared at the ground, moved his feet a little. "Yes, boss. San Diego. Not so far from Mexico, no? MI HERMANA—my sister, she live there."

"Hmmmmm," said Mr. A as he turned to look at me again. "Well, if you want to help your uncle by working on the ranch for a while, Yancy, I can pay you a small wage and feed your horse for free. Sounds pretty fair, doesn't it?"

"Yes, sir! More than fair."

"You lived on ranch property in San Diego with the horse, did you?" he asked.

"Uh, no," I answered, thinking fast. "I had my horse at a boarding facility. That's why he's here. I'll save a little board money. We—we're having a family emergency. That's why I came without warning Tavo."

Arnold squashed his cigarette on the pavement and clicked a garage door opener that he pulled out of his hip pocket, and then he climbed inside a black Corvette.

"Thanks, boss!" Tavo called, and the rich guy waved.

The 'Vette resembled an alien eight ball as it silently rolled over the asphalt, and then it was burnin' itself a path all the way out to the road, vanishing fast in the desert until it blended into nothing. And wouldn't it be cool, I told myself, if Mr. A would let me drive that thing? I almost kicked up my heels and hollered: I'M EMPLOYED! SHY'S SAFE! MY NEW BOSS OWNS A CORVETTE! But I held it in.

Tavo picked up Arnold's squashed cigarette butt and tossed it in a trash can. "Okay," he said with a wink. "Now we go work."

I followed him down the driveway, walking fast, like I knew exactly where I was heading.

STILL DAY SIX—

8 p.m.—inside my new trailer home

Horses are work, and I like work, and Tavo got right on it this afternoon by asking me to help. I'm used to hard labor at Frank's stable because Shy gets free board there, and Frank works my butt off to pay for it. Mindless shoveling, stacking, cleaning, sweeping. I am useful on the Triple R.

The p.m. feeding was interesting, measuring special vitamins for certain horses, weighing grain or bran or beet pulp for others. A few horses needed injections. Tavo has got to be intelligent to keep track of it all.

Dinner finally, and Tavo's MACHACA tacos were better than Dad's, and I loved the mild salsa because it didn't make my eyes water.

Now my back presses against plastic-covered beige cushions, my bed for later on where I am writing, always writing, and here I sit with no friends but Tavo. But hey, no Will either. My mom says when you're really down or lonely, think about something pleasant.

So I am thinking about when I was in kindergarten and how my teacher, Miss Lewis, the first love of my life, set up easels with large, creamy newsprint paper. Then she mixed thick tempera paint in empty milk cartons that she told us to save from our lunch trays. One day an independent discovery happened and I figured out how to blend colors after the teacher read us a picture book called **LITTLE BLUE AND LITTLE YELLOW,** which was about two splotches of color that blended into **GREEN**. I can remember the excitement of watching the shades come together when I painted with both hands using two brushes at once. I still see the dips and dashes of reds and blues that leaped into strange purple hues climbing off my gooey hands and drip-filled brushes to travel across this imaginary world created by ME the five-year-old. Dad still has the old newsprint artwork. He and Mom swear that each

101

one is "a masterpiece." My parents framed a few, and the work is hanging in our den along with my more recent stuff. Mom had small plaques made: YANCY APARICIO—ARTIST with my age at the time, and they show my life, frame by frame, a progression of experience and new technique, and sometimes it's like walking inside a tunnel of what I might end up with, all the things I might become, so my pleasant thought right now is our den being filled with more and more of my creations. Maybe my parents will frame some of my poetry with plaques: YANCY APARICIO—WRITER. If I ever go home again. And maybe if I don't.

Tonight when we were sitting beside the small fake-wood table during dinner, between bites I mentioned to Tavo how he's such a great cook, and he nodded his head and made a big grin, and it took over his face.

"Sí, for survive I learn, but my wife, Anita, she the good cook. The two babies, they love Mama's cooking."

"So your family's in Mexico?"

"Sí, VERACRUZ, MUY LEJOS, but GRACIAS A DIOS they no come with me. I have the dangers to come here."

This statement made me curious. Dangers?
Sounded like a good story, and I said, "Dangers?"
out loud, hoping to encourage Tavo so he'd keep
going.

"SÍ, MUCHOS PELIGROS."

He served both of us more Mexican rice.

"So what happened?"

"Well, for come here, Yancy, to LOS ESTADOS
UNIDOS, I pay money, all my DINERO, and hide under
the floor in a big van. The month, it is August,
and the day, it is very hot. Two men, HOMBRES
MEXICANOS, they drive me and four more people.
We are all hiding. We no can breathe under
that floor! And we get to the desert across
border in the U.S., and the men, they yell,
'Get out!' We do this, then they leave."

And what Tavo told me almost made me
choke, and I had to drink my Pepsi to stop the
coughing. "What do you mean, they left?"

So he goes, "I mean they leave us and drive
away. The desert so hot ¡AY, TAN CALIENTE! and
after one day, a man, he is very old this man, he
die. Then comes a car and they see us, and these
people give help to us and call the AMBULANCIA for
take us to the hospital. And I feel very afraid

they send me back again to Mexico, so I run from the hospital. Then after three months I find this ranch, the Triple R, and now I here legal. Mr. Arnold help me to get immigration papers."

Tavo's story forced me to stop eating for a while, and the rich taste of MACHACA and corn tortillas faded off my tongue until the only thing left was a faint saltiness.

"God, don't you hate those men?" I asked. "If it was me, I'd be out to kill those guys. I mean, it's like you could've died in that desert. You probably want to destroy them, right?"

The brown-skinned man stared at his wide, strong hands. The wind blasted against the trailer, and he said no. "No time for hate. The life, it is short, Yancy. You understand this? I make up for bad if I do much good, then maybe that help me wash away all the MALO from those men."

And while I considered that idea, the canvas awnings started to flap outside. They were slapping like frenzied drums while the trailer vibrated with the force. I thought about how much good Tavo will have to accomplish in order to meet his goal. I mean, he'll never catch up. Not in his lifetime.

Later on when the rain started, the first rain I've heard since April, the drops battered our metal roof, quick and sharp. Tavo opened the window above the miniature sink, and cold air blasted in like a slap. The scent it carried was parched sand that had been exposed to a small bit of new moisture. Both of us breathed long and deep. My thoughts went to shelter, how Shy and I both have a roof tonight. And Tavo? He didn't tell me what he was thinking. We stood there inhaling something in our universe until, five minutes later, the rain stopped.

DAY SEVEN—
9:15 p.m.—in the trailer

Nights on the Triple R
inside Tavo's trailer
I can feel the stars shift
and I am shifting, too
we sleep against black and purple
where protective clouds cover the sky
and I stain the air on my paper
with art pencils and pens

a new self-portrait emerges
Yancy leaning against Shy
alone
in the night
pale moon
invisible desert
reflections on my
buckskin's
beige coat

Tavo's out front
sensitive and seasoned
he must know about life
I paint his eyes
sad and knowing

I think he's
our guide

DAY NINE—

So three days have gone by since I got here, and I can't believe how much work Tavo accomplishes around this place. It's like he's always exercising horses or irrigating the pastures or driving to town for more equine vitamins or calling the vet or cleaning manure out of the stalls or grooming horses or bathing them or leading them down to the arena so the trainer can work with them. It's crazy, and I can barely keep up with the guy.

Every morning we get up at 5 a.m. and my breath explodes into bursts of steam while Tavo and I feed twenty classy Arabians. Ol' stocky Shy is lookin' out of place beside these fine-boned animals, and I tell him so, but I don't think he cares a bit.

Today after breakfast, I was pushing a heaping manure cart down the center aisle where the light slides in and dust floats through. Someone near the entrance walked by in a hurry and I was able to notice something interesting—a very nice female ass in tight jeans. Too bad she turned the corner, because I didn't see much else. Except for

107

long black hair. My question of the day:

WHAT IS ON THE OTHER SIDE?

What Tavo said a few seconds ago when he glanced over my shoulder: "Good work, MUCHACHO. ¡MUCHO TALENTO! But where is the face on this MUJER?"

And he grinned while I turned a bright shade of red.

DAY TEN—
9 p.m.—inside the trailer

Today as part of the training schedule, Tavo and I went on a trail ride.

"You gotta nice quarter horse! I hope this filly learn something from Shy today." Tavo had to shout over the wind while Mr. A's four-year-old Arab pranced around, her body all tense and her light flaxen mane and tail whipping against the air.

Shy kept trudging forward, head down, calm and focused, and when a plastic bag fluttered like a trapped bird against a yucca plant, he didn't even look at it. The spooked filly snorted at the bag and darted to the side, hopping over a small cactus, but Tavo didn't move an inch off that

English saddle seat. He had both hands busy, one controlling each rein since he was using a gentle snaffle bit in the filly's mouth, riding with a two-handed English style. I wondered out loud where he learned so much about horses.

"MI PAPÁ, he have horses and I help when I am a small boy."

"But you've got great hands on that snaffle bit! And you're riding English. Did your father teach you that?"

"No, this I learn from Mr. Arnold's trainer. He show me each thing for the horses, and so I learn. And you? You sit on the horse good. The trainer, he ride like this. Centered riding, no? Who teach you?"

"Oh, my friend back home. An old guy named Frank."

About then Shy stopped and raised his head, fixating on something in the distance. Good eyes, ol' boy. Check it out!

This galloping white horse, a beautiful mover with a rocking-horse gait practically floating across the slopes, melting into the trail. I couldn't see much of the rider, just long black hair, but I could tell she was riding bareback. Plus I was pretty sure, even so far away, that the hair matched that nice ass I spotted yesterday. And then she disappeared.

Tonight, about an hour ago, Tavo and I went out to blanket the horses in the barn.

"Maybe I talk to your parents," Tavo told me, and then he fastened a buckle under a mare's belly, and God, she pinned her ears and raised a hind leg before I could react. "Look out!" Tavo shouted, and I was already leaping away when her shod hoof missed my shin by an inch. "You gotta pay attention around the horses," Tavo said with a slow shake of his head, and by then

I'd forgotten the comment he'd made about my parents until he said it again.

I started thinking, **SHIT. WHY DO WE HAVE TO GO THERE?** But instead I said, "If you contact them, Tavo, they'll make me go home."

"Listen, son, maybe this not so bad a thing for you to go home. You need the school, no? Maybe your brother, maybe he get better by now."

And that made me laugh. "No way, man! Not him. Other kids with the same disorder, maybe they get better, but not Will."

Tavo stared at me hard. "Okay, for now, you stay. I gonna give you a break. ¡PERO NO ES PARA SIEMPRE! You need to think about things, Yancy. Think about your parents. They love you MUCHO. They miss you MUCHO. And they love the other son, TU HERMANO, ¿NO?"

I didn't answer. I just latched the stall door so we could move to the next horse. Tavo pulled a red blanket off a metal bar. "Your papa, he no use the belt?"

"Ha! You mean like give Will an old-fashioned whippin'? I wish he'd use the belt, but the method they learned discourages parents acting in anger. I'm not kidding. Like my dad is an angry guy sometimes, but he's really not over the edge. Not ever. I mean, he used to smack Will once in a while before they taught him all these Anger Control Techniques. But now my dad has to keep himself calm around my brother. He's supposed to give him time-outs, which did help for a short amount of time when Will was younger, but if you ask me, Will behaved better when Dad paddled him now and then."

"And your MAMÁ? She is good with your brother?"

"Well, my mom is way calm and quiet and she wants Will to do good, but she's not much of a disciplinarian. He sorta gets away with a lot when she's in charge. Listen, Tavo, my brother's smart and he's sneaky like a . . . like a . . ."

And then Tavo laughed. "COMO UN ZORRO. In English? Like a fox!" He paused, then hooked the buckles on the red blanket underneath the horse's belly. "You think you got a bad life, Yancy, but your mama and papa, they have a more bad life, no? This boy is their son just like you. They want the best for him even though he is so sneaky like a old fox."

WILL'S NO CUTE LITTLE FOX, I started to

say. **HE'S A KOMODO DRAGON.** But before I could get the words out, Tavo started singing a hearty ballad in Spanish. With no one to talk to, I got involved in a weird mental conversation. My Self spoke to My Other Self.

YANCY 1: Tavo's gonna send me home one day. If he does, Will might stuff me in a meat grinder or something.

YANCY 2: God, I hope not. I mean, shit! Those parents of yours don't pay you any attention. You're invisible, dude.

YANCY 1: Exactly. And now this guy Tavo here, he seems to think my parents have a "more bad life." Worse than me, even. Crazy, huh?

YANCY 2: It's worse than crazy. It's demented! I'm on your side.

YANCY 1: But maybe Tavo has a point. I mean, who wants a son like Will? It's not very rewarding.

YANCY 2: Maybe not, but your life totally sucks. That's my opinion. You're the person everyone should feel sorry for.

After blanketing the last horse, we headed back to the trailer. Tavo paused outside the door under the dim light and he tapped his toe in the leaves. I watched his boots.

"It don't make sense," he said, "but maybe now I start to understand and maybe when I think of horses, then it make sense this brother and you." The toe tapped faster. I wondered what he meant. I didn't say anything. Finally Tavo continued.

"Back in Mexico, MI AMIGO, he raise many horses and sell them to his friend in U.S. for racetrack. One day he show me two horses. He tell me that this one is smart and very quiet and he learn fast. He is the horse that gonna win the race. Next my friend point to another horse, same color, almost a twin, a beautiful blood bay, MUY BONITO. Now this animal, my friend say, this one NO ES MUY INTELIGENTE. He never listen and he is very stubborn. He is not gonna make it out the gate when the race start. 'Look here at my arm,' my friend tell me. He roll up his CAMISA and he show me a big, red, ugly bite with horse teeth marks. 'That son of a bitch bite me!' say my friend." So then Tavo turned toward me and took hold of my shoulders. "And you know what, Yancy? These two horses are brothers. Same sire, same dam. The bad horse, he is one year older, and the young horse, he is the smart colt. So when I think about this, then maybe it make sense. Sometimes the good breeding? All the training? All the care? It no count for much. Maybe God is the one who form the personality. He is the one who have the plan."

So, Adventure Journal, maybe shit just happens. We're like the horse brothers, Will and me. He's not okay. I am. And that's just the way it is.

DAY ELEVEN—
12:00 p.m.—sitting under a tree by the pasture

The other side
(SOMETIMES Y' GOTTA LAUGH!!)

fifteen minutes ago I saw the nice ass
AGAIN
and I almost ran it down
by **ACCIDENT!** when the manure cart
went *THUD*
and a girl spun around glaring
"Watch it!" she yelled
and when I saw her features I actually choked
to keep from laughing straight out loud
in her outrageous, space alien, graphically
illustrated FACE

So finally! I met the mystery woman. Dracula's Bride started checking me out all over, top to bottom, and since she's a little rich girl, I felt like crawling in a corner or something.

"So who are you?" she asked, and the lids on those two-hour-paint-job eyes fluttered. I decided that she might actually look beautiful under all the mess, and she's got a hot body for sure, no denying it. Then she glared at me just like Will does. I started thinking, **WILL! DUDE! I HAVE FOUND THE PERFECT WOMAN FOR YOU!**

"Do you have a name or not?"

"Sorry. I'm Yancy. Tavo's nephew."

DING! The expression on her face transformed into something I think they call SUPERIORITY, and her eyebrows wrinkled, and she squinted at me like she was staring at a bug under a microscope. I could feel myself being lifted by giant tweezers, examined, and then filed in this lowlife category, the one reserved for Mexican laborers. Hired Help. Maybe from her POV, if Tavo's my Uncle in Real Life, wouldn't I be a so-called second class-citizen?

"Well, I'm Grace Arnold, but my friends

call me Grass. Just don't use that name around Daddy!"

"Mr. Arnold's your dad?"

She stared at me like I'm dog poop after that question, so I figured the answer must be YES. Then I asked her why she's not in school.

"Got kicked out."

NOT a huge shocker. "So you're not getting an education, then?"

"Bein' homeschooled—by Daddy." Big sigh, exaggerated-roll-of-the-eyes type of stuff. "And what's **YOUR** excuse? Why aren't **YOU** in school?"

Hmmmm, pretty good question, so I told her how San Diego has this year-round schedule and we're offtrack right now until after Christmas. Then I said, "And your friends call you Grass because . . ."

She shook her head and started to walk away, kind of slow (and sexy). Kept walkin' and lifted a ziplock baggie of marijuana out of her pocket. Mumbled, "Cuz I love to smoke it." Still moving, without looking back: "You understand, li'l cowboy?"

Yeah, baby. I do understand! I do realize you are Big Trouble, capital B + T, for sure.

When Grass marched around the breezeway

corner, this gust of wind whipped her black flared pants against her skinny ankles while all that hair circled her head like wild loose feathers on a binge. Ooooooh, the perfect explosive Manga character! And I bet I dream about her tonight.

DAY TWELVE—
4 p.m.—tack room

Fun Day. All morning Tavo let me drive the tractor, a small skip loader with cool gears and a scoop on the front. Mr. A wanted four potholes fixed in the driveway, so I hauled gravel to the holes, filled them in, and then leveled everything. For a while it was way confusing, and the scooper turned upside down and all the gravel would come pouring out, but I coped. Tavo said I did good.

Operating Mr. A's tractor got me to thinking about driving. Thinking about driving immediately made me remember Will and his ridiculous reward chart and how much he loves cars. Cars! Waaaay dangerous, especially when I'm trapped inside one with him.

Six months ago, just Mom and Will and I were flying south on the 405 to one of his shrink appointments, and he flashed one of his most adorable smiles, asking Mom if he could please NOT go to therapy that day. Mom said he HAD to go, so Will tried The Nice Approach again because that works so well with Mom but she held firm—parents of children with conduct disorder must do that—hold firm—even though maybe it's not in some parents' personalities to act that way.

"I'm sick of the motherfuckin' shrink!" he told her, kind of punching his fist against the dashboard, and Mom said sorry, he'd just lost another point on the reward chart for saying a bad word.

"Frankie invited me to go bowling with him and Jarvis. I'd rather be there!" Will's voice, so edgy, making my heart beat too fast and maybe Mom's heart, too.

"Calm down," she said (good job, Mom), and then she told Will that he definitely needed to keep this date with the shrink, and after that Will started breathing hard. Then he unsnapped his seat belt and . . . BAM! His left foot rammed the brake pedal and I knew we were gonna die, and our 75 mph Toyota Prius swerved and we almost hit the center divider, and then Mom screamed just as the car straightened and skidded to a stop. My brother laughed because this was soooooo amusing, and then he fastened his seat belt again.

After that day, Mom never drives Will anywhere.

DAY THIRTEEN—
11 p.m.—in the trailer

So now I'm huddled in my trailer bed, and a few days have gone by since meeting the Impressive Miss Grass. Yesterday her chauffeur drove her someplace, and when they returned I watched him unload a zillion shopping bags from the trunk.

Tonight the wind is howling like a wounded creature, and Tavo gurgles these snoring gusts that are louder than the wind. The whistling and whining gets inside my brain and I can't sleep in this trembling metal box, and the clock on the counter clicks, reminding me that I've gotta get some rest.

Something just grabbed my attention, and it's the cell phone sitting above me. Home. My link to it. Fully charged, ready to use . . . should I? Should I call them? Tavo thinks my parents have it worse than I do. But if I talk to them, what will happen? Will I lose my resolve and break down and beg them to come and get me?

Twenty Minutes Later:

The Phone Call was made inside Shy's stall with Mom answering on the first ring while Shy bumped against me with his nose. How her voice sounded—so weak—and the way she waited, hoping that I would say something, and the silence made me want to cry.

"Yancy? Is it you?"

She asked the same thing over and over. I really tried but I couldn't answer, because my mind was overflowing.

Then Dad picked up our other line, his voice so overcharged, hoarse, like someone whose emotions were out of control. "Yancy? Son? Is it you?" And it was strange, so strange, but I lost the ability to talk.

Mom (tearfully): Where are you?

Dad: We miss you, son. Please come home.

Mom (sobbing): We love you so much.

Dad: Talk to us. Tell us where you are. Did Will do something else to make you run away? This isn't just about the tail thing. Am I right? You need to tell us, Yance. What did he do? Did he hurt your horse?

Mom (blowing her nose): Sweetie, are you safe? Please tell us where you are!

Voice in the background: Hey! Who's on the phone?

Dad (hand covering the mouthpiece): Go to bed . . . it's late . . . and keep your voice down. It's your brother!

Will: **WHAAAAT?** Mr. Perfect finally called? It's about time!

Dad: I told you to go to bed. This doesn't concern you.

Will (shouting): Yance! Mr. Perfect! Can you hear me? How's your stupid horse?

I flipped the cell phone cover—**SNAP!**—and I remembered those terrible words Will hollered after he cut Shy: "Your fuckin' horse is gonna die!" It's exactly why I can't go back. Maybe he'll do it. That's how much I doubt my

parents' ability to control my brother. That's
how much I believe in his insanity.

DAY FOURTEEN—
2 p.m.—on a hill above the Triple R

JUST HAD TO GET THIS IN:

My friends are coming over in, like thirty minutes so I need you to saddle up five horses. NOW.

Yeah? Well, I'm in the middle of something.

So stop— HEY! WATCH IT, YOU JERK!

Oops. Sorry. Didn't mean to drop the horse shit so close to your feet.

STILL DAY FOURTEEN—
1:15 a.m.—in the barn

Tonight after thinking about My Real Home and
My Worried Parents, I ended up doing it again.
This time, when the phone rang at That Other
Place, Mom answered. She talked about how I am
not home where I belong and how she and Dad

miss me and they're very worried for my safety. They want me back! They love me!

Then she explained that my brother just got arrested for shoplifting—what a jerk—took a six-pack of beer from the local 7-Eleven and resisted arrest so they hauled him away for a temporary visit at Juvie Hall. Which is perfect because now I am NOT missing home. Will is the universe at home. But why did Mom sound so shocked about the arrest? I am not shocked. The dude has a beer stash hidden in our garage. He keeps a mini-ice chest out there. When I ask him where he gets all those Coors or Bud Lights or whatever, he just laughs. Mom and Dad have never done a thorough garage search, and anyway, Will keeps a supply of After Beer Mints to help protect The Guilty.

Mom just told me how their support group (the group I call Parents of Completely Wacko Offspring) will meet tomorrow and that her friend is going to speak about a new treatment for conduct disorder. She and my dad are hopeful about this new treatment. And then she sighed.

After this beer arrest, Mom is certain that Will's gonna lose even more points toward the learner's permit. So I'm wondering, will he be lower than zero? Should they make a second chart with minus points? Negative numbers? If they do, then Will can keep going back and back, further and further, and he will be grounded with no form of transportation until maybe he's eighty years old. It's pretty pathetic to picture Will's first opportunity for successful operation of a motorized vehicle to be his electric wheelchair in the Center for Senior Citizens or something.

Then, with her voice all shaking and tearful sounding, my mother explained how Will's issues are not what has her upset. The most horrible thing in her life, the most horrible thing ever, is NOT Will. It's ME. Because I am MISSING. Her talented, wonderful boy, her genius son, her child of light, the kid who writes and paints so beautifully, is gone. Not home with his parents who love him. And then she started to sob, and at last my words came **OUT**.

"Mom! Don't cry. Listen to me. This is way beyond stealing beer, okay? Will said he's going to kill my horse."

And for a minute Mom didn't say anything.

All I could hear was the sound of her sniffling against the receiver.

"He said **WHAT?**" she asked.

"He threatened to kill Shy."

"Oh, but honey, surely you don't believe he was serious!"

So I said good-bye in a hurry, and after I hung up, standing there with the cell phone in my palm, staring at it . . . angry . . . wondering how come they couldn't see the truth. It made me want to punch and kick the wall, and then my anger made me think about my aunt's Chihuahua, Burrito, his tiny body a crumpled heap all curled next to the wall, broken and helpless, his little paws twitching. With Will sobbing, calling it an accident.

Oh yeah, Mom. The truth is not a pretty thing.

Thirty minutes later:

I'm all stretched out on the narrow table-bed, writing this down because my thoughts are worth getting to while they're

FRESH

After I closed the journal and returned to the trailer, Tavo was awake and ready to listen.

"So my brother got picked up by the police."

"AY, what he do? He is in a fight?"

"No. This time he stole a six-pack and ran for it. And you know what? I think they should just keep him in custody because my mom sounds like she's gonna lose it."

"Sure. She got full hands, no?"

"No. I mean, yeah. Yes. She's got her hands full."

And then comes the:

BIG THING!

"Now let me tell you something, Yancy," Tavo said, his voice deep and expressive. "Where I from in my village, we no have the choices the people have here, because if a child is born and this child is not okay he is gonna live with you for life. You understand this? POR EJEMPLO, UNA SEÑORA EN MI PUEBLO, her name is Violeta, and she have a retarded daughter. Now this daughter, she is UN ADULTO and this daughter is maybe forty years old. But Violeta change the diapers, feed her daughter, do everything for her. So when I send money to Mexico for my wife, some go to Violeta for buy food and things she need for this girl. Violeta have a job at her house, to sew flowers on beautiful cloths for the tables. But they no pay much for this work. So we help."

I cleared my throat. "And when Violeta dies? What's gonna happen to her daughter?"

Tavo didn't answer, and the trailer got all cramped and stuffy, sort of like we were trapped inside a sealed casket, and pretty soon Tavo started snoring, so I pressed my face against the pillow for a while, and then I opened my journal.

For some reason I can't think about what's going to happen to Violeta's daughter, but I can think about what will happen to Will and my parents when he's older and if he'll be there following them to their graves, pushing them closer and closer. And I want to write about it, but I'm so sleepy, and my cheek wants to lean against the clean pillowcase and push against a river of things I don't want to know, and it's a flood of shit I can't deal with. Not tonight.

DAY SIXTEEN—

9:32 p.m.—in the barn, leaning against Shy's stall

It is freezing cold on the barn floor where I'm sitting, and my breath comes out like hot steam in the air, and my hands hurt so much I can barely write, but I have to, because I've done it again.

I called home.

So tonight Dad answered. "Hey, son," he said with that special tone in his voice and, God, I wish he was here to hug me and tell me everything is going to be fine, but I held in my words and I held in my tears, too. Then Dad described how boring it is at home without me there, and I stayed silent, and then he tried to cheer me up, maybe hoping I would talk.

"I just invented a salsa recipe, and it's the hottest one so far. Listen to this. Fresh habanero chiles, lemon juice, salt, and garlic. Killer stuff!"

This info made the back of my throat itch. Then Dad explained how Will is back home. Already! The court gave him a break on account of how this was his first offense, etcetera, and they have an appointment in juvenile court the following week.

Then he said, "So listen. Mom told me that Will threatened to kill your horse. He had no right to say something like that, son. Hopefully this is just a phase because he's never been this bad before. Maybe he'll shape up."

SHAPE UP???? ARE YOU KIDDING????

Then Dad kind of sighed, and I remember the exact words he said next: "You must wish I'd get rid of him. Right, Yance?"

I was thinking, *HELL, YES! SEND THE GUY TO SIBERIA!*

But Dad had other thoughts. "I can't quit, son. Maybe it's my stubborn streak. I have this hopeful side, and I can't seem to let it go. I'm doing my best, but I sure as heck don't want him hurting you or your horse, so I guess I'll just have to try harder. I want the poor kid to succeed. Is that so wrong? Maybe he'll become a productive adult and actually make it as a professional race car driver. I want him to have a chance."

And I didn't say a word, but maybe some air came out hard from between my teeth, and it hit against the phone so Dad at least thought I was listening. But I'd stopped listening. I was thinking about Dad's dreams for Will, the fearless race car driver, and how I've got my own dreams. But I can't even enroll in school out here without a birth certificate and shot records and all that other shit they ask for. I'm a ranch hand in training. That's what I've got going for myself on the Triple R.

Maybe Dad read my mind from fifty miles away. "Wherever you are, Yance," he said, "I hope you're okay. You've got so much going for you. Like your education. Your future. You're an incredibly talented kid."

And then he talked about his culture for a while and how important it is for Latinos to Take Care of Their Own, and those words brought on thoughts of Violeta.

So much stuff is starting to make sense.

DAY SEVENTEEN—
2 a.m.—the barn

Nights Like These
hanging with my journal

sharing a twelve-foot stack of hay bales
with the Queen of the Barn,
a splotchy orange cat named Chica

mice race along the back wall
while the kitty leans against me and purrs
I try to focus on mice and cats
giving no thoughts to The Future
but when my pen moves
The Future shakes like a sweet dance club
where strobe lights make me dizzy

Chica rolls on her back
and I tell her:
GO CATCH A MOUSE. DON'T BE SO LAZY
she closes her eyes part way:
PURRRR PURRRR
     YOU'D BETTER GET A PURRRRRRFECT
EDUCATION, DUDE, BEFORE YOUR LIFE
GETS PURRRRRFECTLY SCREWED FOREVER

     SHUT UP, MS. CHICA
     WILL'S FUTURE IS SCREWED . . .
     NOT MINE!
and I lean my head back on the dusty scratchy bales
and by accident . . . I dream

DAY EIGHTEEN—

10:15 a.m.—Mr. Arnold's garage

I hope I don't get caught hangin' out in here, but it's warmer than the barn. And I love the smell of cars. Mr. A has three of them. One is a bright yellow Jeep Wrangler... My fantasy is to fly through the hills in that Jeep. With a girl, of course. But who? Miss Grass? Hell, yeah! We could cruise the dunes and get naked. Or maybe Christi.

She enjoys off-road excursions. Christi . . .
Christi . . . Christi . . . I'd call her, but what's
her last name???? Sciarro? Scirio? I could
contact Gomez, but he knows less about Christi
than I do.

It's not important. Christi wouldn't remember
me. I'm pretty positive about this because most
girls don't like short guys and especially not me.
NOT YANCY APARICIO. Too bad, because
I really miss the way she laughs and how she
reaches up and pushes that colorful hair off her
neck and then swings it around, and those out-
of-bounds remarks she makes are way funny.

The first time I noticed her, I mean
REALLY noticed her, was not one of my
proudest moments. There was this former student
named Francisco, who has Down's syndrome, who
was hired as a noon aide. Francisco worked very
hard to keep the tables clean, and he assisted
the plant manager by picking up trash. So this
one day, Gomez and I heard all this yelling and
laughing five tables over, and there was this
group of Losers tossing wads of paper and food at
Francisco. And he was, like, all dodging the stuff,
looking totally confused. So something in me,

this small inner voice was telling me: *GO HELP POOR FRANCISCO!* and I started to stand up. But Gomez grabbed my arm.

"Are you insane?" Gomez whispered. "Monty's at that table. He carries a knife. Remember?"

And instead of doing The Right Thing, I listened to Gomez, and now as I write about it I wonder if FEAR of Will put me in training for being A Fearful Dude. But anyway, I sat down, and guess who marched toward Monty and his group. This short girl with reddish-orange hair and freckles, and she was wearing a lacy blouse that reached the middle of her stomach when she raised her arms and shook her fists at The Losers.

"Fuck off, all of you!" Christi screamed.

The Losers hooted, and Monty jumped off the bench where he was sitting and yelled back at her. "Fuck off yo'self, bitch!"

But Christi stood solid, so Monty flipped her off, daring her to make a move. By then Francisco was crying, and big tears rolled down his face. Christi turned away from Monty, grabbed a napkin off someone's lunch tray, and handed it to Francisco. The part I liked best was when she wrapped her slender arm around the poor guy's flabby shoulders and led him to an empty table where she stayed until he was ready to go back to cleaning tables.

After that day I tried to sit close to her every Wednesday during our art club meetings. She'd say hi when I sat down and that was about it.

but I'm a big chicken—shoulda
talked to her a long time ago
shoulda shoulda shoulda
bwak! bwak!

STILL DAY EIGHTEEN—
2:00 p.m.—beside the arena

Something strange happened today. I was in the barn grooming Shy and thinking about Christi in Chatsworth, and there's that Grass Hot-Body Issue, and there's that Christi-Doesn't-Know-I'm-Alive Issue. I heard a soft voice. Even though I hadn't heard her come into the barn, it was Grass, whispering to her horse, Ali, in this baby-talk language. She was wearing this knit cap with magenta designs, like from India, with a perfect dark braid slung over her shoulder. And the usual face, of course. Tavo has these brushes for cleaning the barn walls, and I've got this fantasy about scrubbing all that makeup junk off. God, it makes me laugh to just think about it!! I mean, what the hell is UNDER all that crap? So I started to imagine Grass with a naked face, and then with a naked body, while I brushed Shy with long, soothing strokes. Grass kept talking to Ali about whatever, feeding him carrots, and all of a sudden she moved in a quiet way and stood beside me and stroked Shy's neck.

"Hey. How come he's got such a short tail?"

"My brother cut it off."

"You've gotta be kidding!"

"No. I'm not kidding. My sixteen-year-old brother whacked it off one afternoon."

This info got Grass to giggling. "How funny!" she said, still smiling. I didn't get the joke, but at least her black-lipstick smile was pretty engaging. She patted Shy's back. "So what is he? A quarter horse?" Her question sounded like an accusation.

"Yeah. A registered quarter horse . . . and he's fast."

"How fast?"

"Way faster than your Arabian."

"No way is he that fast! You'll have to prove it."

The Gory Maiden almost spit these words, and the black lips grinned in a strange dog-eat-dog sort of way. And it's like the expression on her face was telling me: *I AM THE RICH KID! YOU ARE THE TRASHY GUY WHO WORKS FOR ME. MY HORSE IS IMPECCABLY WELL-BRED. YOUR HORSE IS A LOSER.*

So we made a deal to race our horses. We even shook hands—she was wearing these black mesh gloves with all the fingers cut out, her long fingernails painted black.

So right now Grass is in her mansion, changing into riding clothes. I've groomed and saddled our horses. Oh, and Ali just pooped, so I'd better clean it up before she gets back.

Me Barn Help. Her **PRINCESA**. And Shy? Well, he's pumped up to win!

STILL DAY EIGHTEEN—

10:30 p.m.—in the trailer

THE RACE

Shy takes off blasting forward like a rocket

and when he reaches the far side of the arena his training shines

and we spin around faster than an Olympic swimmer doing laps.

The **PRINCESA** really hates to lose and she sticks her tongue out at me

A silver stud wobbles and gleams smack in the middle of her spoon-fed, spoiled, bratty, rich,

little, sexy mouth

After the race, Grass **ORDERED** me to unsaddle and groom BOTH horses. She said it like this: "Okay, Mr. Hotshot Barn Guy. You can clean 'em up now."

So I saluted her like she's the Captain Major, smiling big, because Shy rocks. After the horses were taken care of and safe in their stalls, I went back to cleaning the breezeway aisle. Grass leaned against the open door of an empty stall and put on a pouty face. Then she lit up a joint.

"Want a hit?" she asked, reaching toward me to pass it over.

I kept sweeping with long, rhythmic pulls, thinking how I tried pot a few times and how the high was really creepy, and I wondered if I was like Will those times when I was stoned and didn't have control. So I said no and explained how I don't do drugs.

"So you're a boring little cowboy."

I can't believe she actually said that, but she did, and then she inhaled again and flicked her ashes in the dry hay, and I stomped on them just in case.

"Yeah, that's me . . . a loser," I said, hoping she'd catch the sarcasm.

That's when she did this wild, hip-swinging walk in my direction, holding her joint to the side. She grabbed the push broom, knocked it to the floor, lowered the navy blue-goo lids over her eyes, and kissed me full on the mouth. God, it tasted like weed. Her tongue poked inside of me, prodding—felt so good, yeah! And my tongue brushed against that silver stud. Both hands grabbed her hips while my body sort of pressed into hers, and I was thinking I could do this all day—maybe in one of the empty stalls? But when we pulled apart I felt my whole life crumble.

DADDY!!

Mr. Arnold—two feet behind us, and his anger sat heavy like a freakin' summer storm where thunder rumbled across his face, and I could almost hear the explosion growl inside his head, and I could sense the ugly thoughts he was inventing, and it made my knees go weak, all loose like my kneecaps weren't connected to anything solid.

"Get in the house!" Arnold yelled, and his daughter took off like a spooked filly while I prepared myself, knowing I was someone who was gonna get demolished, possibly killed. And when the boss grabbed my neck with both hands in a strangling choke hold, this is exactly what he yelled:

"I should whip your ass, you worthless piece of shit. How DARE you touch my daughter! Have you forgotten your place around here, you little SPIC?"

While he screamed, he tightened the grasp on my neck, and no air was getting through, and I figured, hey, what a stupid way to die! HELP! And I prayed that Tavo would get back from his trail ride and rescue my butt, but finally Mr. A let go, with me all doubled over, letting the air rush in, gulping and sputtering, until I could talk.

"Sorry," I said, my voice coming out like a cough.

"**SORRY?** Well, that's just not going to cut it. It isn't over, you little bastard. Not by a long shot." He raged off, the sound of his boots cutting through the breezeway until he disappeared.

I bet tomorrow there's gonna be fingerprints on my skin. As for tonight, there's no way I can clear out my brain. The main word pounding on me right now is SPIC. What kind of person says that? In school last year a dude called someone a spic, and they expelled him.

During dinner I told Tavo what happened.

"The boss, he have the fast temper," he said, winking at me. "Tomorrow? Mr. Arnold, he gonna calm down."

So now it's almost eleven, we're in bed, and I'm spinning with scenarios. I'll never sleep. Not tonight! Grass and her sexy ass, her tongue-filled kiss . . . plenty to dream about there. But in reality? It's ALL over where The Boss is concerned.

I just heard something outside . . . there's
a noise—distant voices . . . feet crunching through
gravel . . . the sound of a fist pounding on our
door.

DAY NINETEEN—
3:11 a.m.—back in my real home in Chatsworth

I can't believe what has happened. I am NOT
hiding in my safe little trailer while I write this.
ADIÓS, little trailer.

First there was knocking, and Tavo jumped out of
bed, fumbling with his pants, fumbling, mumbling,
"¡UN MOMENTO!" the floor creaking as he hurried
to the door, and when it swung open, what
was outside shocked me more than a scary scene
straight out of a Stephen King movie.

changes

they leaped at me and I was in their arms
wrapped in a tangled crowd of everyone's love
"Thank God you're safe!" Dad, like a drowning man
Mom kissing my head my cheeks my eyes
"Yancy-my-Yancy," again and again
I pulled away before I vanished in
all that affection, disappearing in
the truth . . . that I'd missed them
"How did you find me?" I asked
new strength dominating my voice
I heard this indignant stubbornness
and during those few seconds I sensed a whole
new
me

because the old me, Mr. Perfect, would never speak with a voice that strong so I said it again:
"HOW DID YOU FIND ME?"

Dad started to explain: "Mr. Arnold called the house a few hours ago, because he found your student I.D. and tracked us down. We came right away."

"I can't believe that dickhead went through my stuff!" I said.

Tavo frowned and glanced at me, then shook hands with my parents. "Gustavo Mendoza, pleased to meet you. Your boy Yancy, he is a very good boy. He work so hard here on the Triple R, and he say many good words about his FAMILIA."

No one answered or responded. Tavo asked Mom and Dad if they'd like some coffee, and then he folded my blankets and lifted the table into position, and I knew I should be helping, but coffee? We were having COFFEE? With me completely immobile, like an observer taking mental notes, while Mom and Dad squeezed behind the table, folding their worried-looking hands. When Tavo opened the coffee can, it

148

didn't smell wonderful and nutty and earthy like usual. It smelled like stagnant, rancid, dead things.

My feet planted themselves on the linoleum like a horse who doesn't want to go inside a trailer. "I'm not leaving!"

Dad was on this immediately. "Staying is not an option, son." And then he turned toward Tavo: "What were you thinking? You've been harboring a runaway, Mr. Mendoza. What you did is illegal, and I should send the cops over here to take you away."

"Wait a minute!" I shouted. "Tavo saved my life."

Dad's eyes widened.

Tavo set down the coffeepot so hard I was shocked it didn't break. "Sir, I say truth to you and I pray you listen, because your boy Yancy, he is afraid. He need me for protect him and for protect the horse named Shy."

"Yeah," I said. "You can't make me go back."

Dad stared at the floor and then straight at Tavo. Something passed between them. A truce? A bargain? Probably a realization that they were on the same side.

"My son belongs at home with his family," Dad said.

"Shy and I need protection!" My voice was shaking.

Tavo stepped close and placed his hand on my arm. Suddenly I was seeing my vulnerable world through his eyes. And for the first time, I could see it through my own eyes, too. Not through my parents' perceptions. I could see the way I've always lived. Like when I fell off Shy and landed in the gully, alone and scared with no one around to help. That was how my life with Will had always been.

And Dad's expression, so powerless, almost like he could read my mind. And Mom, looking like her life had split in half with her two sons divided. Separate. Two opposing forces.

"For you to feel safe is exactly what we're after," Dad said.

And Mom agreed that yes, of course that's what they wanted.

Tavo's face, so sad and knowing, because who could be blamed for this?

And the timing was perfect, oh too perfect, because Guess Who popped the door open? Will's

gaze, vast and glittering, darted around and
stopped on ME.

"Hey, bro. Whassup?"

Mom rushed to the door, to Will, the other
son, and Dad reached over to touch my chin
with his thumb. "Get your things, Yance," he said
softly.

I didn't move, and I barely even breathed, and
everyone stared, waiting, and it was completely
quiet inside the little trailer except for Will, who
was inhaling in a powerful way, but that's just me
thinking about these details now, putting it all on
paper, and I remember what I said next.

"What about Shy?" Good question! VERY
good question, because I was gazing through the
window and did not see a freakin' horse trailer
behind the car . . . even though the Prius couldn't
handle one. "I'm not leaving without my horse."
My words, sucked helplessly toward my hopeful-
looking father, then soaring off, like maybe out
the door where my mother was hovering over
Will.

"I can trailer Shy to you on Saturday," Tavo
mumbled, staring at his bare feet.

"Oh good," Will said from the doorway.

"I **LOVE** Yancy's horse. I've been missing that horse."

And for a person who might not understand the implications behind his evil mind, Will's sentiments sounded very real and sincere, but to me the words hit hard. They made me remember my new strong voice, and somehow I found it, and the words came out almost like a scream. "That's why I'm not going home! He cut Shy, and I don't want to live with him."

"You should've come to us about that issue before you ran away," Dad said. "And now you have my word that he won't do anything like that again. NEVER again. I promise."

"Like you can change reality," I mumbled.

"Bro!" Will said. "I swear I'm not gonna torment you or the horse."

"I hope you mean that," Dad said, glaring at Will. His voice had this stressed-out, frustrated tone, an extra sting I wasn't used to. And even though my father sounded stern, he sounded really tired, too. Maybe he was tired of the same old shit. Maybe he was all worn out because there was nothing he could do to fix this. Not really. One of his kids ran away because it got so bad.

His other kid has a messed-up brain, and that brain probably won't be getting better. Just like Violeta's daughter, maybe Will is stuck inside himself forever.

Those words of Tavo's: *YOUR MAMA AND PAPA, THEY HAVE A MORE BAD LIFE, NO?* Those words were starting to sink in.

So I gathered my junk and stuffed everything in my backpack. Then I opened my wallet where I'd kept my salary and dropped every penny of it, over a hundred bucks, on the table/bed where I'd eaten and slept and drawn and written and talked and grown for the past two weeks—had it only been two weeks? It felt more like a lifetime, and I'd spent it in the company of the best man I'd ever known.

"The money is for your family," I told Tavo, "and for Violeta's daughter." My voice echoed inside the small trailer, a quiet empty sound, and I knew I was strong because of him. Of course, Tavo said he could not take my money, but I was already outside and the bills remained on the table.

and when my feet hit the driveway
I wanted to fly
become a cloud picture
live in the sky
float around to choose my own shape
and never come back down
and never come back down

The sound of gravel and leaves crunching under my tennies reminded me of the day I'd arrived on the ranch. Back when I was a runaway. Shit. It would be easy to bolt through the darkness, hide in the hills, and return before dawn to quietly saddle Shy, hop on, and blast out of there. I'd find a new trail, ride through creeks and on pavement, so they couldn't track us. I'd create a different life.

I glanced over my shoulder and spotted Tavo standing in front of the trailer. My guide.

"Go home, son," he told me. "Everything is gonna be good."

I didn't move and kept staring at Tavo's image, the glow of moonlight surrounding his solemn form, the only time I'd seen him look completely powerless.

"Go!" he said, his voice breaking.

And while my heart exploded into tiny, aching pieces, we crammed our bodies inside Mom's car. The tires spun on the gravel, and we zoomed down the driveway, and the Triple R became a void. Gone. Erased! Did it ever happen? Because at that point in time, I was just a passenger being delivered to Hell while All That Stuff That Changed Me in Palmdale banged against my chest.

But hey, I've got my journal. I have my REAL thoughts. There were nights on the Triple R when I dreamed about my brother, and I was in this place running and running without going anywhere, and Will was behind me holding a pair of silver scissors raised high, aimed at my back, his expression cold and vindictive. I'd wake up breathing in short spurts, carrying an icy knowledge about the reality of my life. And now I'm home. I have to get past my fear, deal with it, conquer it. I have to find a way to be strong. It's huge, this art of surviving.

Will's here. Will is here!!! How am I going to endure my brother's shit after everything I've learned? Tavo's race horse story jumps into my head, the one about his amigo, the dude who raises horses for the track. One horse was smart and quiet, and he learned real fast. He was a good boy. But the brother horse, the older one, wasn't so smart. He never listened. What a stubborn horse he was. He actually bit his owner on the arm.

So which horse is gonna win the survival race in our family? I guess we'll have to find out.

DAY ONE—
Friday—2:14 p.m.—at school

I'M STARTING OVER—THIS IS DAY ONE AGAIN inside the famous Adventure Journal.

I'm sitting in my history class, and I don't have much to write about except that I've been looking everywhere for Christi and haven't seen her. I still have this sweet image of Grass and her hips and that belly button ring, too. She lusted after me. Is that not what happened? (Even though she treated me like some kind of worthless Latino loser.) But I guess that kiss made me "a hottie" in her eyes, right? Okay, she was STONED . . . but still . . .

Maybe before my sexy self-image fades, I should try it out on Christi.

STILL DAY ONE—
Friday—11:25 p.m.—home

Gomez was way excited to see me, and of course he got the details in full color about my adventures, loving the parts about Grass, even though she caused My Ruin, making me describe the make-out scene about fifty times. Then he told me how this is the perfect day for me to be back home, because of his brother's birthday party. I should be there tonight, Gomez insisted, because no one else our age was gonna attend, being as his brother Ramón is a senior, which meant that Gomez had absolutely no one to hang with. And the most excellent information was that Gomez's mom and dad are visiting relatives in Mexico.

When Dad dropped me off he wanted to speak to Mr. Gomez to be sure the party would be well supervised, but I said not to worry because Mr. Gomez was in the backyard cooking hot dogs, and

for sure he and Mrs. Gomez would keep an eye on us. Dad believed me because I'm Yancy the trustworthy kid, and then he drove away.

Almost immediately, Gomez and I heard how there was going to be a birthday piñata, and we were like, "Whaaaat?? A piñata? Are you eight or eighteen today, Ramón?" And I was imagining a rainbow star-shape or maybe a blue-and-yellow donkey, but now I'm laughing to myself as I write this, and I hope Mom and Dad don't hear me LOL. Anyway, when Ramón's friends brought the piñata from the trunk of someone's car to hang it from a branch, we couldn't believe it. The piñata was not a star or a donkey. It was a penis. Super detailed, and everyone busted up almost rolling on the ground, and the girls were all saying, "Oh, how disgusting!" even though they took turns trying to smash it, too.

So I told Gomez that this could be a rite of passage thing like this male QUINCEAÑERA event, a new Latino tradition. By the time my turn came up, the balls were almost falling off, so I gave them a powerful whack with a small baseball bat while I was blindfolded. The guys had to wear a pair of ladies' super-size panties for a blindfold, and I couldn't see a thing, although I tried to peek through the lace. And **WHAP!** That sucker split open, and everyone started shouting, "Yancy! Dude! You are the MAN." It was like I became an important person for about three seconds, which is something new, because in my house Will is the King of Getting Attention and I've always just been Mr. Perfect. The party people scrambled across the grass because the piñata was completely filled with condoms and candy but I didn't bother trying to grab any. There was only enough time for me to drink one beer and eat some chips with guacamole because I had to rush home and get there no later than eleven, so I grabbed an extra beer for the road and disappeared.

Inside our house, when I glided past Will's room, he leaped in front of me and sniffed the air. "Holy shit, li'l bro, you actually need an After Beer Mint!" I kept going and Will yelled, "Dad! Mom! You guys had better check out Mr. Perfect. I think he's starting to get a life."

And for once I guess maybe Will was right.

DAY TWO—
Saturday—3:05 p.m.—home

My parents keep warning Will that they'll take away his allowance and his reward-chart progress if he bothers me or goes near my horse. Maybe my brother needs his drug money or beer money so he can self-medicate, because except for the excellent Beer Breath Moment after Ramón's party, he's been staying out of my way. I can do this!

Early in the morning, Tavo pulled up with the horse trailer, and I climbed inside his Magical Music Wagon, and we headed down to Frank's. Shy backed out cautiously, and I caressed his soft black nose, and he said, "Hello, Yancy!" by wiggling his whiskery upper lip on my shoulder, and my yellow sweatshirt got a sloppy hay-colored-horse-snot smudge. God, I've missed those smudges.

When Tavo drove me home he wanted to know how things were going with my brother. I told him so far so good. And who knows? My father believes miracles happen all the time, and maybe he's right. Will might shape up.

A few minutes later we were parked in front of my house, and Tavo glanced at me with that thoughtful way he has of looking at a person, sort of right into the place where their soul hangs out.

"I come here from Veracruz," he said. "There I pick coffee but get laid off. My friend, he come here with me to the U.S. and bring the wife but just one kid. His other kid, he have to stay in Mexico with Grandma. They cannot afford for two sons to cross the border. They have not enough DINERO. This very hard for my friend, decide who stay and who go, but the adults, **THEY CHOOSE**, and one boy stay in Mexico, and the other one come to the United States."

"What are you saying, Tavo? That my parents have to choose between Will and me?"

"Maybe," Tavo said. "Maybe one day it come to that."

And while I'm writing about it, a funny scene just flashed into my mind. If it ever does come to that, I've got the perfect method:

FAMILY POKER NIGHT

When we climbed out of the truck and hugged each other, I could smell horses and sagebrush on Tavo's work shirt, and for a split second it felt like some of his strength poured into me.

"I'm really gonna miss you," I told him, wiping my eyes with my forearm. "I mean it."

"You gonna be okay, Yancy Aparicio," Tavo said, his voice soft, and then he was wiping his eyes, too.

He turned and hopped into the truck, slammed the door, and started the engine. A familiar Latino ballad came on the radio when the truck pulled away from the curb. Tavo's voice joined in with so much Life and the scene created a feeling that hit me hard, sort of like watching something you love a lot die and disappear forever.

DAY SIX—
Wednesday—8:40 a.m.—school, 1st period

Today Will's first sign of showing his real self, the Old Will, popped to the surface when he slammed his body against my chair during breakfast.

"Oops!" he said in a real loud voice for Mom's benefit. But she was stirring eggs on the stove and missed it all.

Then he glared at me the entire way to school. I ignored him, not for long, because my school is close to home. Dad drove off with my brother still safely sealed inside the car, so Will could attend his public school special education classes five miles away at a place where they give him a one-on-one T.A. to keep him on task and out of trouble.

I can coexist if Will behaves this way. I mean, it's been six entire days without major conflict. No horse threats. That's the best thing. Mom and Dad have noticed and that race car is all the way up to square number eighteen. Good job, bro.

I am mainly in a good mood right now, and even though I've spotted Christi at school, I would've felt like a geek going over to say something to her. Maybe today it will happen. After school. At Art Club.

STILL DAY SIX—
Wednesday—4:30 p.m.—Frank's stable

Art Club did take place and Christi was there and this is what went down:

She arrived at 3:15 and I noticed how her colorful hair was all captured and pulled back, and her face looked clean and fresh with that little gap between her front teeth. I'm not into female fashion, but her dress showed the top part of her boobs, and it made me a little nuts. I figured that I should probably admire her from a distance, like always, like before, but there was that kiss from Grass with her tight ass, where she was grinding her body into mine. (And if her dad hadn't caught us . . . ??) It makes no sense, but that memory helped me stare at Christi. Long and hard, with a look-over-here message behind it. She noticed! And it's gotta be a sign how at that point in time, I wasn't invisible anymore. Because she walked over to where I was sitting.

"Hey," I told her.

"Hi!" Big smile. "So where have you been, dude? I've heard rumors."

"What kind of rumors?"

"Like you ran away from home. Stuff like that."

So I told Christi that yeah, well, I'm back now. And then I said something that a forty-year-old dork might say, like it's great to see you or something, and Christi put on her purple-framed nerdy-cool glasses with rhinestones, which called attention to that little diamond on her nostril.

"I think you got more cute while you were gone," she said.

And I was thinking, *WELL, THE GORY MAIDEN SEEMED TO THINK I WAS OKAY.*

I gave Christi what might've been a sexy smile, and she straightened the top part of her black dress, and I decided that she smelled like some kind of flowers. Then Jordhan came in with her tight pants and kind of fell in the chair beside Christi and dumped a Burger King bag on their table.

Christi peeked inside. "You know I love fries, but they are so full of FAT."

Jordhan peeked in, too. "Yeah, they are so freakin' good! And I've got lots of catsup to go with."

Christi shrugged her shoulders and dug for a fry and passed the bag to me, and I grabbed a handful. Just then Antoine, the Art Club president, called us to order. Acting impulsively, I ripped a sheet out of my spiral notebook and picked up my favorite pen, the kind that doesn't leak on airplanes, and I Didn't Think About What I Was Going to Write and This Is What Came Out:

CHRISTI
SO WHAT ARE YOU DOING FRIDAY AFTER SCHOOL? WE COULD MEET AT STARBUCKS OR SOMETHING. Y.

When I handed her the paper, Christi read it.
Then, with an exaggerated motion, making her
eyelids flutter, fanning her face with her left
hand, she tucked my note inside the top part of
her dress.

"I just **HAD** to do that," Christi whispered,
pressing her shoulder into mine. "On the classic
movie channel last night? This actress kept a
stash of cash in her bra."

"Very dramatic," I said. "Maybe you should
audition for the school play."

The agenda moved along endless and non-
stopping, the note sweating hotly against
Christi's boobs, an image that made it impossible
for me to concentrate on business. We formed
work committees to discuss the upcoming plans for
the fall performance and our role as Art Club
members to design and paint the scenery, until
finally Antoine hollered, "Meeting adjourned!"

On the way out, Christi leaned against me.
"About your note?" she said, resting her palm on
her chest while I tried not to stare. "Starbucks
might be interesting. You can tell me about your
adventures from when you turned up missing.
I'm s'posed to help Jordhan pick out some shoes

167

at the mall after school, so I'll meet you at Starbucks around four. Okay?"

And for the first time, being home and not on the Triple R is starting to look almost amazing.

DAY EIGHT—
Friday—5:30 p.m.—Starbucks

Christi had to head for home already, but I'm still sitting here with my journal, steamy coffee scents everywhere, and it's so cool to be writing. Like an author.

Anyway, after school, even though I took my time getting here, I still arrived early, hands sweating from nerves, worried she wouldn't show. But she did show around four fifteen, out of breath, her cheeks all pink.

The main thing Christi wanted to talk about was my running away adventures.

I told her everything but left out the parts about Grass, and never did explain a thing about my brother. Christi said Tavo sounds like the best person who was ever invented. When she had to go home, she kissed my cheek.

"Let's do this again. Soon," she said.

That was my favorite part of today. It was a feeling I used to get as a kid, like wishing for something for Christmas and getting it, only this gift was actually better than my expectations. Christi . . . Christi . . . Christi . . .

DAY NINE—
Saturday—10:35 p.m.—in my room

The phone started ringing a few minutes ago, and I answered, figuring it was Gomez, picking up fast before it woke Mom and Dad, but the voice I heard was not Gomez.

"Hey, Yancy, it's Grace. You know, Grass Arnold from the Triple R? I just wanted to apologize, um, like, let you know how sorry I am that Daddy called your parents."

It took a second for my brain to grab hold of who I was talking to. "I'm confused," I finally said. "You kinda treated me like trash most of the time I was working on your dad's ranch, and now you're calling to apologize about getting me busted?"

"Yeah, well, I kissed you. Remember?"

Her words got me shaking my head. What was I supposed to say?

Grass kind of coughed, or maybe she was inhaling weed. "Now I feel terrible about how you lost your job. It was my fault, and I hope we're still friends."

A vision fired through my brain. I could

actually taste her lips and that sex-driven tongue, but immediately the taste got clouded by a different picture of Miss Rich Bitch ordering me around, living in a mansion where she believed her birthright made her superior. But I didn't tell her to fuck off.

"Look," I said. "You can make it up to me."

"Like how? Tell me and I'll do it."

"Ask Tavo to describe his adventures about coming to America and crossing the border. Maybe you'll understand how immigrants—"

"Jesus, Yancy," Grass said, interrupting me. "There's another reason why I called. Um . . . well, Tavo doesn't work here anymore. I don't know where he is."

Did she hang up first? Did I? For sure it didn't matter. All I could think about was Tavo.

DAY TEN—
Sunday—4 p.m.—home

The sun came out this morning; there was a cold breeze, but not too bad. Dad headed out on his Harley right after breakfast. And I took off for

171

Frank's to help him unload and stack two tons of hay. After that, I rode Shy for about an hour on our favorite trail.

When I was almost home, I noticed Will and his friend Jarvis unloading stuff from Jarvis's truck and carrying it inside the garage. Scary. I went through our front door, and Mom was in the den reading a book and listening to music with her headphones on. I grabbed a piece of cold pizza and headed for my room.

Big question of the day: **WHAT WERE WILL AND JARVIS UP TO?** My room's not far from the garage, and I could hear them laughing and banging things around, dragging huge stuff across the floor, hammering, laughing some more, until finally the hinged door out front closed with a loud squeal. So I sneaked inside the garage to investigate, hitting the switch for the overhead fluorescent lighting. Nothing. Everything seemed perfect, so what was all that noise about? Finally, after crawling around on my knees to get behind Dad's workbench not far from the beer-stash ice chest, way behind our old exercise bike, I noticed an eerie glow. I kept crawling.

Whoa! Weed! Six baby plants growing in a

long, narrow planter with special lights attached low on the wall, extending over them. And a dark cloth draped around the sides to keep everything way hidden. So if someone were to find out about this, which would be a huge possibility, being as Will has at least zero good judgment in his brain, and for sure every messed-up druggie at his school probably already knows that Will Aparicio is harvesting weed . . . well, if that should make the cops come over here, couldn't my dad get in a bunch of trouble? Maybe even lose his teaching job? That's what I was thinking this morning. But now? I figure doing the right thing is not always smart.

Anyway, just as I headed inside, Dad banged through the front door and tossed his helmet in the closet. Strong New Me took over immediately, which I now recognize as Zero Good Judgment, because I actually thought it was my job to wear the Nark Badge in our family.

"Dad," I whispered, glancing toward the kitchen where Will and Jarvis were scarfing up the rest of the pizza. "You'd better follow me to the garage and have a look."

With Dad in the rear, we crawled around out there, and I showed him the evidence, and my father said "shit," and then he ran back inside our house.

"Will! Jarvis! You figure my garage is a perfect place to harvest your pot?" Dad was standing close to Will, yelling in his face while Jarvis backed away, blasted himself out the front door, and then took off in his truck.

"**WHAT!**" Will said, gasping, his eyes all wide and innocent-looking.

"Don't act like you're not aware of what this is about." Dad's voice, way harsh. His face? The shade of a tomato.

Will's eyes got mean, and that's when I realized that, hey, what the fuck was I thinking, tattling on a sociopath? Was I fucking stupid or what?

Dad watched my brother stare me down. "Leave Yancy out of this," he said.

"Why leave Fancy Yancy out of this? He wanted to get involved in my business, so now he's in way over his head!"

I wondered . . . *IS THIS IT? IS THIS DAD'S BREAKING POINT? IS HE GOING TO FORGET*

HIS SELF-CONTROL AND POP WILL A BIG ONE? But no. Dad took a deep breath.

"Okay," he said, and took another breath. "I've had it this time. First, we're going to trash those plants. I think the garbage disposal will work just fine. . . ."

Right then the phone rang. Mom answered. She peeked around the corner and informed Dad that Mr. Garza wanted to speak to him.

"Mr. Garza's son is failing, so I have to take this call," Dad told Will as he hurried away. "We'll dispose of the you-know-what as soon as I'm finished."

The second Dad disappeared, Will kicked the side of my foot. "You're gonna pay for this."

"What do you mean?"

"Well, Mr. Perfect, it looks like I'll be forced to poison your horse."

"WHAT?"

"I'm gonna put rat poison in his hay, you asshole."

My heartbeat went crazy, but I told myself to stay calm, act reasonable.

"Dude," I said, trying to come up with logic Will might understand. "When those plants mature, for sure our garage will reek of marijuana. And if somehow Mom and Dad were to miss that odor, which I doubt, if you sell it, the police might find out. Dad could get in trouble."

"Trouble? Ha! This is how I deal with trouble."

Will spun around and lifted his long, light brown hair. On his neck, against the white skin, bold gang-style lettering:

Permanent. The letters all in black, and it must mean something, but I didn't get it. Will straightened himself, stood tall, smoothed his hair, smiled big like a genuine nice guy.

I took a few steps toward my room. "Interesting tat, bro, but how come you want your neck to advertise death?"

"Because death rocks. It's written in the words."

"What words?"

"The lyrics, stupid. Like that song 'MANGLED AND DYING.' You know the part I mean? When

176

they sing about the world exploding, they go, 'Leave it in your head and the blood is theirs instead . . . Oh, death rocks, my friend, yeah, death rocks.' I write the lines down, and I read them about a thousand times, and I analyze what they mean. And I live my life that way. That's what makes me tick, Mr. Perfect. It's exactly how I am."

"I wish I could figure you out. Did they change your meds or something?"

"Noooooo, of course they didn't. Changed 'em myself."

"Yeah? Well, leave Shy out of it. You poison my horse, and I'll poison you!"

Will laughed again, a weird sound that gave me chills. By this time, Dad was off the phone, and he pulled my brother into the den so they could tell my mom about the latest fiasco.

That's when I left, running to the stables, pounding on Frank's back door. After I told him everything that went down, he scratched his bald head and told me not to worry.

"Yancy, I'll be on my toes. I won't let Will near this place."

I was thinkin', *YEAH, RIGHT, LIKE HOW*

ARE YOU GONNA ACCOMPLISH THAT?

"You do realize horses weigh a thousand pounds," Frank said, studying my expression. "Compare it to a rat. Can your brother afford enough rat poison to hurt Shy? I doubt it."

So, feeling a little better, I hurried home and locked my bedroom door and called Christi to ask her about a concert that's happening in the school auditorium in a few weeks.

"You sound sorta strange," she said.

"I do?"

"Yeah, like you're upset."

"Not really."

"Yancy, I can always tell when someone's world is crashing."

"How?"

"From personal experience."

I waited.

"My personal experience is something I never talk about, but I'm gonna tell you. It happened when I was little and my dad used to beat up my mom. The last time he got violent, I was twelve, and it was **HORRIBLE** and she went to the hospital. My world pretty much ended."

"I wish we were talking face-to-face so I could

hold you," I said, concentrating to make my voice come out normal. "So where's your dad now?"

"He moved to Canada when he got out of jail."

"At least he's gone."

"Yeah." Her voice, a whisper.

Before I could stop myself, there I was explaining my family issues, telling her the Will Stuff. When I described my brother, she got all quiet. I could feel her attention, especially when I talked about The Threat of the Day.

"God, Yancy," Christi said. "No wonder you ran away." Then she suggested I'd better get a plan to deal with Will's shit.

After we hung up, I wondered about our conversation, and how telling Christi about Will had made me feel kind of relieved. Not so invisible.

STILL DAY TEN—
Sunday—9:45 p.m.—in my room

Phase I in getting a plan needed to start with The Parents. First I checked on Will, who was playing video games in his bedroom, and then I made my way to the kitchen. The air near the garbage disposal smelled like a fresh marijuana pie had just been digested. In the den, I peeked through the sliding glass door; Mom and Dad were sitting on a wooden bench, warming their hands by our fire pit. A cozy twosome. Safe. So not afraid.

I hurried outside.

Mom glanced up. "Sweetie. We were just talking about you."

"You were? I bet you were saying how I'm such a great kid. How I'm a perfect student, well behaved and all that."

My voice had a sarcastic tone behind the words, and it made Mom frown. "No. We were saying how everything is way out of control around here. If you decide to run away again, I'm going with you."

That made me laugh, but my parents weren't smiling.

"We didn't realize how scary things have been until you ran away," Mom said.

"How could you not realize? Will's a monster. I grew up with a monster in the house. I mean, have you seen the new tattoo?"

"Tattoo?" Mom's eyes widened.

"Take a peek at the back of his neck. But worse than that . . . Will just threatened to poison my horse."

"Jeez," Dad said, his face gone pale, glancing at Mom. "That was part of what we were talking about." He cleared his throat. "Don't take this the wrong way, son, but would you consider moving in with Aunt Toni for a while?"

I could barely answer. "**RECENTLY DIVORCED** Aunt Toni? With the crazed ex-husband and her pack of toddlers? Also in desperate need of a free babysitter? And what would happen to Shy if I moved to downtown L.A.?"

"You could board him at the L.A. Equestrian Center. It's got to be expensive, but our peace of mind would be worth it," Dad said.

"The Equestrian Center is in Burbank. It's not even close to Aunt Toni's! Plus I'd have to change schools. Leave my friends."

Mom's suggestion was almost as lame. "How about your grandparents? You could move in with them."

"No! Sepulveda's closer than L.A., but it's not nearby, and I'd still have to transfer schools. And they're not zoned for horses, either. My vote is to make **WILL** move someplace. Send **HIM** to Aunt Toni's. Let **HIM** live in Sepulveda with Grandma and Gramps. Or cart **HIM** off to ABUELITA'S house in Arizona. The farther away the better."

Mom and Dad shook their heads in unison.

"No one wants Will," Mom said. She started to cry.

"Yancy, you think we want you living away from home?" Dad said. "It's an impossible situation. Try to understand."

My mind was spinning, reeling back to the last story Tavo had told me, the story about the immigrant couple with two kids. They had to choose, and one kid got left behind. It was obvious my parents had reached that point, and the winner was NOT going to be me.

I rushed inside the house before they could say anything else.

DUDE, YOU HAVE TO GET OUT . . . YOU HAVE TO GET AWAY FROM THIS CHAOS . . . BUT NOT TOO FAR AWAY . . . NOT TOO FAR FROM CHRISTI, SWEET CHRISTI, WHO UNDERSTANDS WHAT IT

FEELS LIKE WHEN SOMEONE'S WORLD
IS CRASHING.

DAY ELEVEN—
Monday—12:00 p.m.—school cafeteria

During English, Period 2, our Word for the Day all scrawled on the board by Mrs. Bentley, who is NOT young and definitely NOT cool, but she wrote a special word for me, like she's got ESP or something: **A N G S T.** We had to copy the definition, mainly a list of synonyms: fear, dread, worry, apprehension, distress, anxiety. And while I wrote the info in my Composition Notebook, all filled with doodles in the margins and the strange drawings in the middle of my notes, something rang true. Maybe this was MY tattoo. MY word.

If my brother is DEATH Tat Boy, then maybe I should become an alternate hero. Defend the guys who get picked on, right? Protect the fearful, stressed-out, apprehensive dudes of the world. Like myself. My first mission? Conquer Death Tat Boy. Grind 'im into pulp!

I pulled out my compass and touched the sharp
point. A lot of kids carve stuff on themselves;
that's the kind of shit Will might do. So
I thought again and dug for my markers, the
permanent ones. My choices:

red—like blood when it hits the air
blue—in the veins, flowing and honest
maroon—internal organs— livers!!
black—vampires and bats and Grass Arnold
yellow/orange—Christi and hairweed

It marched across my left forearm, and it was very fascinating, not boring like whatever Mrs. Bentley was going off about, and I was staring at it and realizing how VERY cool it looked on me.

Gomez, from the desk behind, draped himself over my chair so he could whisper in a hissing sound that scattered a little spit: "Arm Art—sweet."

And now, when I stare at the wandering, slick, colorful creation, it's exhilarating, but it still does not erase Will's threat of rat poison or the creepy discovery of his DEATH tattoo, or my parents sending ME away instead of him, and it's all a reaction, like dread. Exactly like the definition says.

And now at lunchtime I wear that word and it's my badge.

DAY TWELVE—
Tuesday—5 p.m.—Frank's porch

Today I rode Shy down some side streets in a residential area to reach the trails, and passed a house with a sign ROOM FOR RENT taped to a yardstick and stuck in the dirt. Perfect! So I tied Shy to the fence and peeked over the gate. Huge—almost half an acre. Room for a horse back there, plus no fancy landscaping to get ruined. Shy could wander around and not get hurt, even though chain link isn't the safest thing for horses, but he would be okay.

I knocked on the front door, and a hairy guy wearing a wife beater opened it while some vicious-sounding dogs went off behind him.

"Shaddup!" he yelled, and these two pit bulls lurched forward, bashing into the screen. But I smiled anyway and prayed the screen door was strong.

"Hi. I saw your sign out front."

"Sure. Let me put the beasties in their yard, and I'll show ya the setup."

"Oh. You keep the dogs in the back?"

186

"Usually. Their doghouse is on the porch out there, so these two pretty much rule the property." One of the dogs nipped at the screen, leaving some slimy drool on the surface. "Shaddup!" The man pushed against the dog's neck with his knee.

"They look like nice pets, but, um, I guess I've changed my mind. Sorry to bother you."

"No problem!" He grabbed the animals by their collars and dragged them backward so he could slam the door. They were still barking when Shy was three houses away, with me remembering Frank's horror story about a pit bull killing a miniature horse a few years ago.

DAY THIRTEEN—
Wednesday—10:25 p.m.—our den

Art club was another Christi laugh-a-thon, because this time Jordhan and Christi were talking about bath bombs, something I had never heard of, but their conversation interested me and I felt glad I'd assigned myself a seat next to Christi. Look at the fascinating shit I got to learn about—putting a bomb in your bath! They described how bath bombs actually explode with fizzing and bursting and sending forth of bubbles and scents and confetti. My imagination was going wild, crazy out of control with pink Fourth of July eruptions that covered the wall and ceiling and Christi's reddish-orange hair and white skin, and all the freckles sparkling with sexy bath bomb contents.

Christi interrupted my oh-so-pleasant thoughts when she stretched her arm over and stuck it under my nose. "Smell this," she ordered.

"Huh?"

"Just do it."

So I took a sniff and it reminded me of the flower scent I'd noticed at the last art club meeting, and getting so close to her little freckles and the tiny hairs on her arm was just too much to handle. Almost.

"Well?" Christi asked.

Jordhan, the echo: "Well?"

"Hmmmm," I started, and then I was kind of scratching my chin like a scent guru or something. "You smell like flowers, Christi. And hearts?"

That got her giggling, and it made me glad

I'm dark in my complexion, because if I was blushing it wouldn't show all that much. When Christi adjusted her peach-colored T-shirt, I glanced away and noticed the ANGST on my brown skin, which was starting to fade. So I got right on it with the markers, and it was bright and glorious and exciting. This time I added a few flames around the edges with gold and silver. Christi noticed what I was doing, of course, and she frowned for just a second, and something invaded her face. I sensed the angst of her life in that frown. She touched my shoulder and told me it's beautiful, my Arm Art, and asked me to make her a tattoo, too. But first she needed a word, and she thought for a while with her chin in her hands. Then she sighed.

"Just do ANGST like yours, but with more goth to it," she said. "With bold edges, okay? And instead of that yucky yellowy orange color, do the darkest of greens."

Sliding, oozing, sex-crazed pens went into motion while I mapped out Christi's gothic angst, resting my left hand on her forearm to steady it, wanting to understand her feelings, whatever horrible shit she'd lived through for twelve years with her violent father. **TELL ME ABOUT YOUR ANGST,** I wanted to say.

"Do me tomorrow at lunch," Jordhan said, sending jealousy vibes in Christi's direction through narrowed eyes.

After the meeting, Christi pulled me to the side. "How are things at home?"

"Not good. I'm gonna find a room to rent close by. Something with horse corrals so I can keep Shy with me. Only problem is, Will lives in this neighborhood. Not too safe. Know what I mean?"

"Yeah, I do. After what you told me, you need to be careful." Christi wrapped her arms around my neck and kissed my cheek while I stroked her soft hair.

And then tonight, one more thing to contemplate, a package Mom left on my bed. Inside I found this beautiful hand-embroidered, colorful tablecloth. Awesome. And a postcard of a 1920s vintage reproduction from old Veracruz with a sepia street scene of a Mexican cowboy sitting on a proud-looking horse. After dinner, Dad translated the postcard message for me while he sat on my bed.

"Tavo says not to worry, that he's back

home in Veracruz. They're constructing a new factory near his house. He flew down there and got a job as a laborer. His wife and kids are very happy, and they would love to have you visit. He asks about Shy and wonders if you ride every day. And he says Violeta got your money, and she wanted you to have the tablecloth. She embroidered it by hand." Dad picked up the cloth and gently touched the intricate stitches. "So, tell me, Yance. Who's Violeta?"

"Oh. Well, Violeta. She's a lady who lives down there in Tavo's PUEBLO and she has to take care of her grown daughter, a low-functioning adult."

"And you sent money to her, son?"

"Yeah."

"That was a kind thing to do. You're a very special person, Yancy. I hope you know that."

I walked toward my window, visualizing Tavo's good-natured features, his light brown skin and gentle eyes, his careful, quiet movements around horses, the peaceful rhythm he creates in a barn when he walks about.

"I wonder if the score is even yet," I said.

Dad wanted to know, what score?

So I told him about that private thing Tavo has going where he's trying to wash away the bad in the world from when he came here illegally and got dumped off in the desert and almost died.

And then I said, "But it's weird how he doesn't hold grudges and how he tries to get over stuff by being good. I think that's why he helped me, Dad, to be good and to erase some of that horrible experience from his mind. Does that make any sense?"

Dad stood and moved beside me, staring out the window, speaking kind of to himself. "Yeah, it makes a lot of sense. If a person goes through life feeling angry and bitter, that person is just not going to have a good life. Do you understand that, son?"

I studied the street below and spoke softly, kind of to myself, too. "Yeah. I think I understand. That's why I want to be just like Tavo."

But now I'm writing about it and I realize how saying those words was just me spouting off some wishful thinking. I mean, maybe I'll never make it to that place, that Tavo-place-of-perfect-existence. My house is like the desert where Tavo was left to die. The difference is, he got away. Tavo escaped, and then he forgave the bad dudes. Me? I'm still stuck in the desert.

DAY FOURTEEN—
Thursday— 7 p.m.—in the garage

So I've been searching online, scanning craigslist, buying the <u>Recycler</u> and the <u>Daily News</u>, trying to find a room for rent that also has a horse corral. It's a rare discovery in Chatsworth. I decided to NOT tell Mom and Dad about my quest, at least not until I find something. At least they've backed off on their idea to make me live with relatives.

Today everything seemed okay at the stables when I arrived after school. Frank moved Shy to the barn where the stall has bars across the front. He added a chain and padlock to the heavy, sliding door. Frank is definitely staying on Will Alert. Me, too.

But once I got home there was something on my bed, a white paper folded neatly, all sitting on my pillow. I figured maybe Mom or Dad left a message or something.

But no. Nooooooo! A note scrawled at the top:

YOU HAVE NOT SUFFERED FOR MY LOSS OF HOMEGROWN INCOME

RAT POISON IS TOO COMPLICATED, YOU RAT-FACED JERKOFF. THIS IS GONNA WORK BETTER!

Below the words—all real and gory and in full color—printed off the Internet—a horse being slaughtered.

So I ran back to Frank's, feet pounding, thudding and rhythmic, but solid—*GET ME TO MY HORSE—GET ME THERE—PLEASE GOD, KEEP HIM SAFE.* I sped up Frank's driveway, into the barn, running to Shy's stall, relief pouring through my body when he poked his velvet nose against the bars. The lock seemed secure. All was fine. But was it?

Maybe not, because my hands were shaking so bad I could barely get the key in the padlock, and when the chain fell to the ground, the noise was metallic, final, like the chains I wear in Will Prison. And I rushed inside, pressing against Shy's neck until my face was buried in his mane and the coarse hair fell over my forehead, and I breathed in the scent of Horse and a thought came to me, then: *IF PEACEFULNESS HAS AN ODOR, THIS IS IT.*

My horse stood so still, not moving to finish his hay, not chewing, not snorting or stomping his hooves. He waited patiently while I got it out. In sobs.

When I walked home, my feet moved slow. I could not loosen up. I could not smell the possibility of rain even though the sky was dark and crowded with boiling, black clouds. Me and my thoughts, hiking through sludge. How impossible would it be for Will to cut that heavy chain on Shy's stall? How impossible? Would he do it? Could he do it?

Inside our house it was darker than the skies and empty. I plopped myself in the first chair I came to in the kitchen and that's when I noticed my word: ANGST glaring, shouting, screaming at the top of my worrisome, apprehensive, distressed, and anxious mind. It needed blood, art blood, pen blood, drops of red ink dripping off the bottom.

And maybe I was concentrating too hard while I drew the bloody teardrops, and that's why I didn't hear Will come in, and of course he had to observe what was going on.

"Cool!" he said, like he was way impressed. "Yeah, dude, love that blood. But what's angst? Does it have something to do with oral sex?"

Dad came in next, on his way to the bathroom. Completely missed the art show.

Will grinned at me. "Did you get the informative little photo I downloaded?"

I pushed past him, my shoulder shoving hard against his, lunging through the door to my room, retrieving the printout from my bed. As soon as Dad headed out of the bathroom I handed it to him and he saw it, and when he digested the evidence, the raw truth of abuse, I knew he realized the depth of what it meant and everything that photo explained in full color, like the answer to their big question:

WHY DID OUR YANCY RUN AWAY?

And he escorted Will through the front door, and they had a loud heart-to-heart out there, standing beside Dad's classic Chevy, Will shaking his head from side to side, the innocent victim, always innocent, and Dad looking like he was falling over the edge.

But I'm not counting on Dad to resolve ANYTHING. I just spent another forty minutes online searching for a local place . . . any place . . . where a fifteen-year-old boy and his horse can hide. I found one possibility in Granada Hills. If Gomez loans me his motor scooter I can make it to school from there. The ad didn't have a phone number, so I replied by e-mail. They haven't responded.

It started raining about thirty minutes ago.

DAY FIFTEEN—
Friday—9 p.m.—my bedroom

I just checked again and no one has answered my e-mail about the Granada Hills horse property with a room for rent. At least Frank is looking for a different stable for Shy. Plus, with all the recent Will threats, The Parents decided that our family should visit a professional counselor for "a little chat." The horse-slaughter photo happened yesterday, and already the Aparicio family has seen their counselor, so maybe the mental health center felt it was urgent? A sixteen-year-old threatening to kill a horse? Yikes! But regarding this therapy thing, Will said exactly what I was thinking: "AGAIN?" (For once we're on the same page. . . .)

The therapist they assigned is named Angelica (the last one maybe moved or retired or maybe she died), and Angelica is heavyset with short, curly blond hair, wearing a long red sweater and also this bright wool skirt all filled with geometric patterns that made me dizzy. Her voice made me dizzy too, especially when she told us how we were in a safe environment and to please share our innermost feelings in her office.

"You mean like wanting to kill a horse?" Will asked.

Angelica coughed and blinked her eyes.

REACT! I told her silently. *REACT, HONEY!*

Dad wanted to react, for sure. I could tell. But Will knows how Dad usually keeps quiet in therapy sessions—my father doesn't like getting in the therapist's territory. The whole situation made Will smile, his hair fastened in a ponytail, his T-shirt fitting tight on his chest. Will's grin looked way confident because he can size up any adversary in a matter of seconds. Everyone sat there waiting . . . and waiting . . . but Angelica didn't challenge Will's question.

JEEZ, LADY, I wanted to say. *WHAT ONLINE PROGRAM DID YOU USE FOR YOUR DEGREE?* But I just pulled up my sleeve, stared at my forearm, and started wishing that I had my pens—how cool would that be—to darken and brighten a few letters on the ol' ANGST declaration. Maybe I could include Angelica's skirt designs. Her outfit was enough to make anyone anxious.

Finally Angelica asked each of us to please share A Positive Family Story. *A WHAT? A POSITIVE STORY? IN OUR FAMILY? GET REAL, LADY.* But this is what my family came up with:

Dad: "I remember last year when Will was the hero at a softball game. He treated our family to ice-cream cones on the way home."

Mom: "Once when Will was six and Yancy was five, they used pancake mix to bake a birthday cake for me. Well, it turned out very flat and mushy. But we popped three candles in the middle and lit them, and then the boys sang 'Happy Birthday.' They served the cake on my nice dishes, and we ate every bite."

Will: "Last Christmas I got lots of cool stuff like fifty bucks from my grandparents and five new video games, and then I sold two of the video games for twenty bucks each."

Me: "Sorry, but I can't think of a thing."

After my statement Angelica did look way concerned, and she leaned against the back of her chair, which made a strange type of squeak. "Shall we come back to you later, hon?"

I was sitting there, lost in her skirt, wondering about my life. I told her no. Really! I did not have A Positive Family Story. Well, unless she meant that time when Will was in boarding school or when he went to a camp for special kids one summer or perhaps the time I ran away on my horse? Is that the kind of stuff she wanted us to share? Or how about a story that takes place in the future? A futuristic tale? Like when I find a place for me and Shy in Alaska and we move there? That's the positive story I could talk about. My life without Will.

Angelica leaned forward. "Yancy, what I hear is that your life is more positive when Will's not around."

Will glared at our new therapist. "He only said that because he's got shit for brains!"

And then he whooped, an odd, menacing sound that sort of shook the quiet room, and his laughter resembled two alley cats mating, and he was wearing that moody explosive expression we recognized Right Away.

I started shrinking, the invisible son, until suddenly the bomb went off and Will leaped four feet away from the sofa and . . . fuck . . . he started trashing the shrink's office! A bunch of books fell off an end table before Dad could reach him.

Angelica, her face the color of a powdered-sugar doughnut, dialed security at the same second Dad pushed Will out the door, practically lifting my brother with his powerful hands, tendons stretching and tight against the back of Will's neck. Angelica told whoever answered the phone that everything was under control.

Mom breathed this sigh like they say in the novels: A Big Sigh of Relief. Meanwhile, I observed how Angelica's hands were trembling. She was shaking worse than Mom gets sometimes, the way I trembled in the barn yesterday—Will has that effect on people, but hadn't this therapist ever met a kid with serious conduct disorder? Get a life, lady. This is your JOB!

And then Mom and I hiked toward the elevator. The first thing I noticed? Will's eyes, all yellowish under the fluorescent lighting and how much he seemed to hate me.

I turned to Dad. "Are you getting the feeling that our situation is hopeless?"

The elevator arrived with a clunk and a *DING!* and the doors slid open.

"Hopeless is a powerful word," Dad said.

Mom started crying, and we crowded ourselves into the elevator.

Will patted her shoulder. "Gosh, Mom, it's never **COMPLETELY** hopeless, is it?"

Which might be an encouraging thing for him

to say, but the sarcasm in his voice was thick like paste.

We made it home from the shrink's office, and the instant Dad and Mom leaped out of the car, before I could grab the door handle, Will leaned toward my ear.

"Bro. I need twelve dollars. Today!"

"Forget it. I don't have that much money. Leave me alone!"

Will smiled, a pleasant grin, and gave me a playful punch on the jaw. "Have it your way," he said. Then he flipped his head forward and his hair draped over his face until all I could see was his word . . . DEATH

DAY SIXTEEN—
Saturday—11:48 p.m.—my bedroom

Such a nice beginning—Mom let me drive her car to school. Well, with her in it, of course. The Art Club scheduled a special work meeting in the auditorium this weekend. We have to finish painting some scenery the carpenter volunteers built for the drama club play. It was especially perfect because Christi happened to be hanging out on the sidewalk in front of school, and she noticed that I was behind the wheel.

The painting activity went well because Christi and I got to work on a sign for the wharf scene, and then she had an idea that we should add a seagull, so the project turned out excellent, because we carved the gull out of cardboard with an X-Acto knife and painted it all realistic. And then we had a little accident. . . .

After we cleaned up (sorta) I invited Christi to walk over to Shy's stable. She insisted that we stop at a market first, so she could buy some carrots, explaining that this was our low-fat lunch, plus it was also a bribe for my horse because . . . guess what?! She's afraid of horses.

"Don't worry," I told her. "I won't let anything happen to you."

When we got to Frank's, I unlocked Shy's stall and introduced my beautiful guy to Christi. She said hello, but stood way back in the corner. After I buckled the halter and snapped on a red-and-white lead rope, we took him to the round pen and turned him loose.

"Have you found a place to live?" Christi asked.

"Not yet. I've been waiting to hear back about this room and corral in Granada Hills, but it's probably rented. Maybe Frank has something for Shy because a friend of his runs a boarding place and she's expecting a stall to open. She wasn't sure. She's going to call him when she finds out."

Christi inched her way over to Shy, and he quickly planted a famous horse-snot smooch on her paint-spattered T-shirt (directly in the middle of her left boob—good aim).

"Yuck!" Christi shrieked.

"He loves you. What can I say!"

"Yeah? That was a horse kiss? He should have a reward, right? But I left the carrots in the barn."

When we opened the round pen, all of a sudden my gut did one of those shocked elevator drops, because Guess Who was sitting on a green plastic chair near the far side of the hay shed. With both feet propped on a small table and chewing the end of a long stem of hay.

Christi stared at Will and he stared at her, and then he stood real slow and walked over to say wassup. And Will kind of winked at me like he approved of her or something.

"What are you doing?" I said. "You're not allowed around Shy. Not for any reason."

"I need that twelve dollars. Came to collect."

"Why don't you just get over it, Will?"

"Because it ain't over! And I'm sorry, I don't wanna hurt your horse, but I guess I'm gonna have to."

Will jogged a few steps to the round pen and pulled the latch on the gate. And even though according to Tavo's race horse story I'm the calm and quiet horse, the HERMANO that's supposed

206

to win the race because he's so smart and learns so fast, I wasn't sure I could be that animal. I wanted to be the horse that beats the shit out of Will. I knew I could do it. He's huge, but I'm wiry. He's fast, but I'm faster.

Will headed straight to Shy, bending over to grab Frank's lunge whip off the dirt, the one that cracks the air with a loud snap to move a horse into free lunging. This whip is **NEVER** used for hitting horses. Frank doesn't do that. But Will?

My brother raised his arm, and the tip of the whip flicked the air, which was Shy's cue to lunge, run in a circle close to the rail, something he'd been trained to do whenever that whip moves. I blasted forward, pouncing on Will, hitting hard. He lost his footing. Like a slow-motion DVD scene, the whip sailed up and landed at the round pen's edge. Shy raced by, leaping over it, hooves thudding on the soft sand. Will and I almost went airborne to get there, side by side, struggling to reach it first. Shy kept cantering around and around, circling fast, a one-horse merry-go-round. I slid through the dirt, my fingers brushing against the stiff handle, but Will dove forward, grabbing my knees; we both tumbled, dust scattering, fists connecting. Shy kept going. Fast! In our direction. Christi screamed in the distance.

"Whoa!" I yelled, and Shy slid to a stop.

Will and I were on each other again, pummeling, punching. We couldn't breathe through the anger, and God I wanted to tear him to shreds, and when I kneed his stomach he hollered, and somehow I wrestled free and jumped up with the whip in the air like he'd raised it at Shy. I made it snap. CRACK! And something in me cracked at the same time and I wanted to beat him to death. To death! Until he became a shapeless mass of mush. Will rolled away, propelling his body through the sand until his back pressed against the metal bars on the pen, and for that fraction of a second he couldn't move, couldn't escape. His face exposed and fearful, with me in charge of the whip. Me in charge of The Power.

"Go ahead. I dare you!" Will shouted.

His words were hard to hear over a horse in the barn that started to neigh—a loud, piercing cry. Agitated. Way upset. It brought me back.

Transformed me into my real self, the calm and quiet one, the smart brother. The winning horse.

I flung the whip over the fence. "Just go home!" I yelled.

In a second he was gone, crawling through the metal bars, staggering off, slinking away like a pissed-off coyote. Christi stood at the gate, her lips all frozen-looking. I walked toward her and Shy followed.

"Shy has to be moved today," I said. "I'm asking Frank where that woman lives, the one with the stables not far from here. Maybe I'll persuade her to let me have the stall even if it's not available."

"Can I go?" Christi asked.

"Yeah. I'm thinking we'll lead Shy over to wherever she lives."

By this time Shy and I were standing side by side. Christi opened the gate, and I could see that little space between her teeth so clearly and the small diamond on her nose with those golden flecks in her eyes. I felt her strength, and it made me stronger; the knowledge propelled me forward, and I held her face in my hands. We closed our eyes and kissed.

Kissing Christi wasn't so much like that kiss I'd shared with Grass. This was a soothing kiss that turned me on, yes, but there was a powerful current that flashed between us, too.

"Whoa," Christi said when we pulled away.

I didn't say anything. I reached for her hand, and everything in my life felt good for a change.

Then we took off, looking for Frank. We told him the plan, and he wanted to come along.

"The owner is a funny ol' gal," he said with a wink. "Name's Miranda, from Texas, about sixty years old. She'll make room for your horse even if she doesn't have it."

So the three of us walked Shy about a mile toward the hills on the other side of Mission Boulevard. The stall wasn't available, but Miranda agreed to let him hang out in her arena.

"I don't suppose you have a room for rent?" I asked.

Miranda told me no, she doesn't board humans. For me, though, the main disappointment was how her corrals and barn weren't clean like Frank's, and when we left, the way Shy whinnied, a real sad sound. I could tell he already missed Oreo, his pony friend.

IT'S JUST WRONG.

While we were walking back to his place, Frank told me to bring my stuff over and sleep on his couch. "You'd better stay out of Will's path for a while," he said.

Christi gave Frank a gentle punch on the arm. "That's very nice of you."

"Yeah, Frank," I said. "Thanks, buddy."

"Hey, Yancy, don't thank me. You're gonna do all my dishes and mop a bunch of floors, so maybe I'm not all that wonderful."

Once we were back at the stables, Christi called her sister, who arrived a few minutes later. They gave me a ride. Then I was bolting inside our house, our exhausting house. And when I hollered for my parents, they came racing from the kitchen, preparing themselves for the latest heap of news. When I got to the whip part, Dad started running down the hall, and we barged into Will's room.

"It was just a joke!" my brother shouted. "I'm not gonna hurt that stupid horse. Why don't you grow up, Yancy?"

Dad lunged, eyes bugging out, arms swinging through the air. But Will rolled to the side, diving off the end of the bed, and then he was gone, straight out the open window. (There he goes!) We heard the gate that leads to the front yard slam shut, and when a car backfired and started on the street, no one reacted. . . . Will can't drive.

Can he?

Instantly we were through the front door, all three of us. Shit! Dad's fun car, the classic, the one he stores with a cover on it, that car went squealing off, exhaust spilling from the tailpipe, engine roaring, and when a station wagon turned the corner, driving slow but crossing in front of Dad's 1958 Chevy, there it was. Will didn't seem to be paying attention to the station wagon or the stop sign.

Then there was the sound of it, metal on metal, and all of us running. I didn't want Will dead. "Kill Will" was over.

And when we got there, his head was all bashed in, and he was crying, but he was alive, and now he's in the hospital for observation. Two nights minimum. It's a big mess. At least the other driver is fine.

My head aches for Will. My arm aches because

it has to keep writing all this crap and it makes me realize how tired I am of everything that goes on in this family. Just like Mom and Dad. I'm tired, too.

I think this journal is gonna decompose or explode or burst into flames from all the shit it contains.

DAY SEVENTEEN—
Sunday—10:00 p.m.—home

With Will in the hospital doing fine so far, just a bump on his head, a few stitches, and a broken arm, I'm able to sleep safely in my own bed and not at Frank's. Then today I visited Shy at Miranda's, the new place. He stared at me like maybe he wonders why I've let him down this way. Why can't he live at Frank's? Like he deserves some kind of an answer that a horse can relate to, only I don't have any answers. Maybe it's like a marriage, this relationship of Shy and me.

It reminds me of the marriage at home. My room's right next to my parents' bedroom, and when I walked past this evening, I could hear parental angst.

"It's too big of a job for us!" Mom was saying.

"Baby, we can't give up." Dad's voice, all strong and pleading.

(My thoughts: WHA—???? C'MON, POPS.)

Then Dad goes, "Listen to me, Jess. We've worked so hard all these years. Too many years. Remember how Will's shrink wants you to take a more aggressive role?"

And Mom, sounding majorly pissed off: "Oh, do not try to pin this on me, Jorge. For God's sake, just face reality! I used to live in denial, but Will is huge and he's strong, and he's also extremely manipulative. So what do you suggest, huh? Should I take up a form of martial arts? Buy some pepper spray? Invest in a stun gun? And what about Yancy? What about his horse?"

"Yeah. I hear you. I know."

And then a sob or a cry or something. Dad's? Mom's? Mine? I couldn't find the source, so I turned and quietly rushed into the bathroom, where the water went on full force, and it ran and ran down the drain, cool and clear, soothing, running deep, a city waterfall with the faint odor of chlorine and chemicals splashing over the angst decorations on ME, until finally the voices stopped.

DAY EIGHTEEN—

Monday—8:00 p.m.—home

After school, Christi told me that she wants to ride Shy. She has to overcome her fear of equines, she says, and that's the final verdict. So I asked how about today? This is a great day because Will's in the hospital until Dad picks him up after work. But Christi explained how today is bad because she has an appointment at the optometrist to get a new prescription, so I urged her to stay with those crazy purple frames.

I touched the side of her glasses and pulled her close. Her chest pressed into mine, and I was breathing around the side of her neck, and it was calm and safe there, and maybe she felt good, too. When I let go of Christi's shoulders, I stared at the ground.

"So tell me something," I said, glancing up for a second, noticing how the light curved against the clear purple frames. "Have you gotten over the horrible things that happened to you as a kid?"

Christi didn't need to think about it. "No," she answered. "It's always there, like in my dreams sometimes, or when I notice the scar over my mom's eyebrow, or when I watch a violent movie."

Her face looked so sad all of a sudden, and I stared at the ground again. "Sometimes I try to concentrate on the future," I told her. "Maybe I'll become a professional artist, like a dude who can paint these amazing, emotional abstracts. When people look at my work, I want them to feel comforted."

Christi rested her cheek on my T-shirt sleeve. "That's beautiful, what you just said," she whispered.

When we told each other good-bye, I decided to head home and paint a comforting abstract for Christi. But when I got there, Dad was arriving with Will. Bandaged and bruised, his arm in a cast, sort of limping. And him being there made me want to leave. Will yelled some bad words in the bathroom because his reward chart had disappeared, and Dad reminded him how the psychiatrist had emphasized for the last two days that the reward system had become pointless.

"C'mon, there was a car accident!" Dad was yelling. "You're lucky you didn't get hurt worse than you did. Do you realize how fortunate you are that the other driver wasn't injured? And what do you think your insurance rates are going to be if, by some miracle, you get to drive before you turn eighteen?"

So maybe this is the last blow Will has been looking for. Maybe he'll totally lose his freakin' mind and do something radical and end up in jail for the rest of his life.

My stuff is packed for Frank's place. His couch is all lumpy and sagging, but who cares.

And I wonder how long it will take for Will to find Shy's new boarding facility.

DAY NINETEEN—
Tuesday—5:11 p.m.—our kitchen

At school, during my last period, everyone wanted OUT just when my mom walked IN.

"Yancy's leaving early," she told the teacher. Handed him a slip of paper.

Gomez, who sits across from me, stared at my mom with his big brown eyes. "Take me too!" he begged. "Please, Mrs. Aparicio. I wanna get out too." And Mom laughed at Gomez and said no, sorry, even when he knelt on one knee and acted like he was praying to her.

When we got to the parking lot I asked how come she's not teaching yoga today. And why did she pull me out of school? Mom said she took the morning off and so did Dad. Before she has to leave for her afternoon classes, she wanted to talk to me. That's why she came to school early. Mom brushed her hand across my cheek. Then she explained how she and my dad made a decision about something. They made a very emotional decision. Today.

My heart started beating a little faster, speeding up and hopeful, so I asked,

"WHAT DECISION?"

Mom tried to smile and told me she and Dad had phoned the Mental Health Center after Will's car accident. They let the administration know how desperate they were getting. Then this morning, that useless psychologist named Angelica redeemed herself. She called my parents because yesterday she heard about an opening at a facility where highly disturbed teens can live and get their education and a bunch of help, too. Right away she thought of Will. So Mom and Dad notified Will's regular shrink, who called the place. The shrink gave that place his input regarding my brother, and now it has all been arranged, like NOW, today! Which is strange because this place is in high demand, but with my brother being such a critical case and all, he's already there. They put him at the top of the waiting list like ASAP. And Will's there, THERE, in this other place, and he won't be coming home until they say so. And when that happens it might be just for a visit. Plus, another good thing is how this place is affiliated with one of those wilderness boot camps where kids get sent to straighten out their lives, and as soon as there's an opening in the wilderness program, Will's going.

"This was the only alternative. It had to happen," Mom said quietly. She leaned over to hug me.

We climbed into the car and she pulled away from the curb, and I hadn't managed to say anything at all. And when the Prius scooted around a corner, we almost hit a pedestrian, and if I hadn't been feeling so numb, maybe I would've reacted or something.

When we got home, Mom said she had to leave in less than an hour, and she didn't ask me if I wanted a snack like usual. She ran to her room and shut the door and turned on some weird chanting music. But I don't think she was trying to meditate. Not today, because today I could hear these big, gulping sobs even though I was inside my room.

And then I heard the phone ring.

"Dude," Christi said as soon as I picked up. "I bought cheesy popcorn and two Red Bulls and stopped by your last class after school today. Gomez said you left early. Wassup?"

"Something unbelievable went down."

"Tell me."

"Well, my parents actually admitted Will to this place for messed-up kids."

"Good," Christi said. "Well, maybe I shouldn't be glad, but he scares me."

"Yeah. He is scary. You'd think I'd feel overly happy, and I guess I do. This is what I wanted, but . . . I can't explain it. It's like I let my parents down."

"Let them down? I don't get what you mean."

So I explained how even though Will is such a jerk-off it's no one's fault, is it? Isn't his brain chemistry just different? That's what they keep saying, and now I pretty much forced my parents to get rid of their oldest son, the one with weird neurotransmitters, and would I want them to get rid of ME if I had conduct disorder?

"Oh, Yancy," Christi said, her voice all husky-steady-calm-emotional at the same time. "None of this is your fault. Like, when my dad went to jail, I went a little crazy. But you know what I realized? My mom and my sister and I, well, we deserve to feel safe. So do you."

"Yeah."

"You get so used to living one way, like scared shitless, so when a better way comes around, it's . . . it's . . ."

"It's so different, you barely know how to act," I said.

We were both quiet for a while.

"Sooooo," I finally said, "Gomez's older brother is driving me and Gomez to a beach party. Not this weekend, but the one after. Can you go?"

"Sure." Christi exhaled into the phone, and the sound reminded me of ocean waves in the distance.

"After it gets dark, maybe we should take off our clothes and go for a swim."

"Brrrrrrrr," Christi said, and then she giggled, which to me was a very good sign. My theory? When girls giggle instead of answering a question, it usually means yes.

STILL DAY NINETEEN—

Tuesday—9:00 p.m.—my room

Safety

I was under the covers
drinking quiet
swallowing safety
clutching my journal

Dad trudged in
looking like an old soldier
and he sat on the edge of my bed
rested his hand on my head

TOUGH DAY, KID, he whispered
*I GUESS THIS HAD TO HAPPEN
I JUST HOPE YOU KNOW
HOW MUCH I'VE ALWAYS LOVED YOU
AND I'M SORRY, SO SORRY
THAT I'VE LET YOU DOWN
. . . UNTIL NOW.*

the words
I needed for my dad
avoided me

and then I realized
THERE ARE NO WORDS
there's nothing I can say

being Will's brother
goes deep, way below the surface
and it hides in an extreme dark place

DAY TWENTY-TWO—
Friday—1:25 p.m.— school—5th period

Experimental Art
yesterday's art class
9x12
pen and ink
the tip of my pen

SCRATCH-SCRATCH-SCRATCH

rapid horizontal lines
fissures form faces
so many faces
I enter

Creation Mode
mesmerized by Process
hypnotized by Work

who's that bold character
the one in the middle
the one with the determined expression
(and it is **NOT** a face without angst)
jeez it looks like me it-is-me me me ME
and hey, I am **NOT** invisible

DAY TWENTY-FOUR—
Sunday—4:15 p.m.—Frank's barn

Shy has been returned to his regular corral at Frank's place. Oreo the pony practically did a backflip when she saw him. My loverboy horse trotted over, making this low whinny sound, and bumped his nose against hers. After that, we went to visit Will on Family Day.

Will's new home where he's lived for five days was a surprise for me because the place is beautiful on the exterior, all lush and landscaped with fountain mist scattering across our windshield. But when we reached the front door, my dad had to push a button.

> because
> guess what
> it's high security here

Dad talked into a speaker saying how we're visiting Will Aparicio, and then there was a buzzing noise, and I pulled the door open. The receptionist in the lobby had to push another button so we could reach the area where the

226

troubled kids live. All of us had to wear special Visitor stickers. Translation: **DON'T LOCK ME UP IN HERE! I'M WEARING A SPECIAL STICKER.**

Mom and Dad attended a meeting with the administrator, while I checked out things in Will's room, 6B. It had two beds and one was filled with this overweight boy who was snoring with great gulping sputters. Will's bed, empty and covered with a wrinkled blue spread, made me wonder. Where was he? All I could see was a small wooden nightstand, barred windows with a view of the parking lot, stacks of school books, and taped to the wall, his favorite movie poster: **SATAN'S LITTLE HELPER**. He's got a shiny desktop computer in the work area, and through an open door I discovered a toilet and shower—looked pretty clean—not Will's usual style.

So I decided to go out hunting for my brother, and my tennies squeaked on the waxed linoleum in the hall, and I was squeaking along beside bare white walls where the air smelled like a hospital. Then, in the rec room, there was this big-screen TV and a Ping-Pong table way back in a corner and a library area with a bunch of books and magazines and a rock fireplace with fake logs. So I walked toward two huge sliding-glass doors and stepped outside into a sparse garden area. An odor of campfires flew in from someplace, but I didn't see any smoke. The building had a wide cement patio with another Ping-Pong table and a bunch of lawn chairs and cement tables, and dry rolling hills spread beyond a volleyball net and two basketball courts.

What really grabbed my attention, though, was the fence. A very tall chain-link contraption with rolls and rolls of razor wire along the top. An icy wind came up and whipped itself inside my jacket, making my chest feel cold, almost like it was pressing fearless smoke-filled spikes into my skin.

Back in the rec room I noticed a group of boys crowded in a corner, and they were all laughing about some magazine photos. And in a chair by the fireplace a waaaaay-too-skinny girl slouched like she was in some kind of stupor. Two kids started playing Ping-Pong—*BANG-SMACK, BANG-SMACK*. Were they girls? Boys wearing makeup? One of each?

And then I saw him. Across the room,

stretched out on a gigantic black couch. I tried to make myself look tall and smiled when I walked in his direction, but Big Brother didn't even wave when he noticed I was there. His face had started to heal from the accident, his arm still in a cast, now decorated with all kinds of weird crap.

"So how is it?" I asked.

Will seemed hazy-foggy and watched me with ocean-like, sea green eyes, and finally attempted a smile. He sat up and rested his palms on his muscular legs.

"Well, looky who's here. And it is BO-ring in this place."

"Don't you have school and activities and stuff?"

"Yeah, sure, but not on Saturdays or Sundays. The rest of the time I'm in, like, four classes and therapy, and I've got anger management and private counseling. A bunch of crap. Oh, they have weight lifting, at least. I like the gym. I always have to be someplace or doing homework. They watch us constantly. No chances for slipups. Maybe I'll find a few ways to keep 'em guessing."

"But you're okay."

"Pretty much, I think. I mean, the food's not terrible and they have some vending machines with sodas and junk. The bad news is that I already got in a fight the second day when this fat asshole ordered me to hand over my sandwich during lunchtime. But if I don't get in any more trouble, they're gonna let me go home for Christmas. They're real into accountable behavior in this place."

"I guess that sounds okay."

Will glanced around, and when he spoke his voice came out hushed. "They said I should apologize. They want me to apologize to you about the horse."

"You mean for whacking off his tail and cutting him and threatening to feed him rat poison and leaving a horse-slaughter photo in my room? Oh, and let's not forget the whip."

"Yeah. All that." Will yawned and bent his arms back to clasp the back of his head.

And that's when Mom and Dad pushed through the swinging doors, and Dad was saying, "That went pretty well except for the increased med dosage."

Just before they reached the couch where we were sitting, I touched Will on the forearm.

"So, you need anything?" Will pulled away and gave me one of those I Hate You Glares, and he kicked his legs back and forth, bumping his calves against the sofa. It made me think about cats and how they twitch their tails when they stalk prey. But Will is trapped in that place, surrounded by razor wire, and I don't have to be afraid of him anymore. So I stared back, this stranger, my brother, same blood as me. At that moment something finally created this clear sense of reality. Part of me realized that maybe this place might work for my brother. Maybe I could end up with a true HERMANO, a best friend, someone who's not going to pound me into the dirt every chance he gets. And maybe Will IS going to become a famous race car driver way off in the future. There's this mind movie I could design with him looking way cool, all fearless and risking his life, almost rolling his race car when it spins out, and he's a hero in that scene. Will the Big Winner.

But for now, there's this: I am the lucky son, the one with a life and a future. My brother's the one who deserves all the pity.

So Mom and Dad and I said good-bye to Will, and when we left, Mom let me drive her car, and she also let me borrow her new Hands-Free apparatus with the earplug, so I could call Christi.

First thing Christi said: "Did your parents sign your application for the Art Club trip?"

And I told her how they said no problem, they'd love a week alone, and I heard Mom and Dad chuckle. And then I asked about her permission form.

"Of course Mom's all stressed about the sleeping arrangements," Christi said. "But I've actually made some progress, so she'll probably sign the papers by tomorrow morning."

"Death Valley should be awesome in December."

"Yeah. Cactus and dead lizards. Oh, it'll be so cool to get some digitals with my new camera. You know how sometimes you buy an awesome toy and you're all excited about it, but there's this part of you that's saying, like, maybe I should've saved the money and bought somethin' else? Well, I'm not feeling that way about this camera."

And I told Christi that I knew what she meant. I really got it.

The car shot through the hills, and our connection started to break, and she said, "So in the desert, you and me, we'll talk

about our angst . . ." and before I could tell
Christi that yeah, that's a perfect topic, the
phone cut off.

Floating

if I hadn't been driving under Parental
Supervision
I would've floored Mom's Prius,
gutless in my opinion,
to find out what it's made of, alright

the small, shiny vehicle would blast up the
mountain road
it would dart like a fast metal thread
and maybe I'd thrust my head out the window
to feel the force of wind in My Atmosphere
yeah!
and I'd yell something, too
I know what the words would be
the words would fly from my mouth
on a day like this
they would rise like solar balloons
and attach themselves to cloud pictures
I can visualize them expanding, puffing, and
billowing against the purple/blue sky . . .

233

I AM YANCY
AND I'M OKAY
I AM YANCY AND
I'M ON MY WAY

For Mike,
who listens
—S. A.

For Mom and Dad
—N. H.

Text copyright © 2010 by Sandra Alonzo
Illustrations copyright © 2010 by Nathan Huang

Printed in the United States of America
First Edition
10 9 8 7 6 5 4 3 2 1
V567-9638-5-09349
Library of Congress Cataloging-in-Publication Data on file.
Reinforced binding
ISBN 978-1-4231-1898-5
Visit www.hyperionteens.com

SUSTAINABLE FORESTRY INITIATIVE
Certified Fiber Sourcing
www.sfiprogram.org

THIS LABEL APPLIES TO TEXT STOCK